CHASING DEATH

DETECTIVE DAHLIA BOOK TWO

LAURÈN LEE

Thank you, Josh!

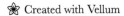

PROLOGUE

The frigid incoming tide of the lake's edge kissed her bare feet. The water lapped against her freshly manicured toes. With each sloppy embrace of the lake, a shiver surged down her spine. Seagulls cawed and swooped overhead while the sun hid behind a dusty cloud, darkening the beach. The shadows mimicked the haunting inside her head. The ghosts she couldn't escape. They followed her here.

Her legs carried her past the tide kissing the beach, lined with twigs, driftwood, and the occasional piece of sea glass. Behind her, a faint voice called out, but she couldn't hear it; she wasn't listening. The sand beneath the water squished in between her toes. A minnow brushed past her bare calf.

Thunder rumbled in the distance, masking the voice behind her that grew stronger. Goosebumps covered her arms from her frail wrists to her freckled shoulder blades. She didn't mind though, she was already numb to it all. Numb to the world, numb to the pain. She couldn't escape the voices any longer. She'd succumb to them instead. Maybe then, it'd get a little quieter.

The person on the beach hollered at her to stop, but she ignored them. She couldn't stop now.

The lake's murky water tickled her neck. It wouldn't be long until it was all over. Her arms instinctively circled in the depths of the icy surface as she couldn't feel the sand with her toes anymore.

Splashing sounded in the distance. Someone dove into the water from the beach. She took one last deep breath and slipped below the surface. Her lungs begged for oxygen. Within moments, hands gripped her arms, but then it all went black.

ONE

I pulled apart the curtains in my living room to expose the threatening storm clouds rolling in off the river. With my Ashford PD mug, I curled up on the windowsill, wide enough to fit my body if I folded my legs and didn't move around too much. I sipped my Earl Grey tea as thunder rumbled overhead. Pressing my forehead against the glass, I delighted in the coolness of the window against my skin. A black figure moved out of the corner of my eye, and I smiled.

"Come here, Salem," I cooed to the rescue cat I adopted a week ago.

Salem trotted toward me and leaped onto my lap without pretense. I scratched his one remaining ear as he purred. After returning back to my new home from my first home, the loneliness of my apartment rattled me. I was alone but also haunted by the ghosts of my past that wouldn't let me be. I figured, why suffer alone when I could find someone else on their own and bring them here?

Salem, an older street cat, held the title for the local shelter's longest resident. I couldn't let that be his legacy, so as soon as I saw him and his battle scars, I knew he had to be mine. The volunteer at Find Your Purrever Home gazed at me with a raised eyebrow when I asked to meet the black cat.

"Are you sure? We have several other younger cats who need homes too," the twangy teenager offered.

I politely declined and asked to see Salem. The teenager, with jeans too tight and her ponytail too high, brought Salem out of his kennel and handed him to me. As imagined, he was a *purrfect* fit for me. Both of us wore our scars proudly on our sleeves, or in Salem's case, his paws.

I hadn't had a drink in twenty-two days and several hours. Each day, I grew a little stronger while my cravings slithered away. I didn't believe I was a true alcoholic as I never had issues prior to Zac's death, but I didn't want to dance with the Devil again just yet. I wanted to get my life together first and foremost.

Last week, I rejoined the gym and forced myself out of bed every day before the sun rose to work out. I pushed myself for a minimum of two hours a day while I worked with a dedicated trainer. Rami was new to the area, and I ended up being his first personal training client. Rami and his family emigrated to the US from Afghanistan about a decade ago. They started in New York City, but eventually wanted a slower pace, so he found his way to Ashford.

He helped me find my physical limits and exceed them on a daily basis. He never let me quit mid-set and kept me motivated by throwing out every inspirational quote in the book. Not to mention, he gave me a badass protein shake recipe that I made after every session.

Now that my physical health was getting back on track, I had to spend more time focusing on my mental health. I kept myself as busy as I could, but sometimes, the loneliness and heartbreak set in. Often at night or during the time between errands, I'd think about how much my soul missed Zac. I couldn't help it. As soon as I woke up, I thought about him, and he was the last thought in my mind before falling asleep. My heart begged the universe for solace, but it hadn't been granted quite yet. Salem helped comfort me some, but I craved human interactions. I wanted the sparks of passion Zac and I fanned each time we were together.

And, when I wasn't drowning in melancholia, I couldn't help but think about Noah. The first boy I ever loved turning into a murderer, and I didn't see it coming until it was almost too late. He could have killed me. He would have if he had the chance. The very thought of knowing someone you once loved wanted to end your life was not a pleasant one.

Then there was the note I found when I returned from Keygate. The loose-leaf paper, now wrinkled and worn from my touch, sat on my coffee table with a splatter of coffee stains. But, the ink was visible and screamed at me from across the room.

Hi, Elle,

You don't know me, but I know you. I also know Zac. In fact, I'm the one who killed him. That dirty pig deserved to die. The world is a better place without him. You better be careful. You could be next...

Yours truly,

Tiger

Who was Tiger? How did Zac become involved with him? Was he in the Jagged Edges? Part of me wanted to walk up and down the streets of Ashford until I found the answers, but the detective in me knew I couldn't be so loose with an investigation. I had to come up with a plan first. I hadn't had any luck in solving Zac's murder before I left for Keygate, but maybe now that I was back, things would be different. Now that I had my head on straight, I could dive back in.

I stroked Salem as I finished the remaining dregs of my tea.

Today was my day off from the gym, which left a gaping hole in my schedule. I'd already cleaned the apartment, picked up my groceries, showered, painted my toenails, and meal-prepped for the next week.

Now what?

My cell phone vibrated in my hoodie pocket, which caused Salem to leap from my lap. "It's just my phone, silly," I said to him, but he stalked away regardless.

I looked at my phone, and my heart skipped a beat. My hand quaked as my finger reached to answer the call. "Captain Dennison?" I asked with a squeaky voice.

"Elle," he said softly.

Most detectives or law enforcement agents couldn't say they thought of their captain as a father figure—but I could. Joshua Dennison groomed me from the moment I passed my exam. He said he saw something in me and would make sure I rose to the level the city of Ashford deserved.

"Hi, how are you?"

Salem trotted back into the room. He leaped back onto the windowsill and curled up at my feet.

My stomach churned and my shoulders stiffened as I held the phone to my ear.

"I'm doing well; how are you? I haven't heard from you in a bit, but word came through about your time in Keygate. Are you alright?"

"I'm fine," I said, ignoring the fact that I hadn't been fine for a very long time.

"And, uh, how's the other thing?"

I sighed. "You mean my drinking?"

Dennison cleared his throat. "Yeah, how's that?"

"I haven't had a drink in weeks," I said as I puffed out my chest.

Back in Keygate, I was convinced I didn't have a problem. I was just doing my best to cope with all the death in my life. If it weren't for Noah nearly killing me because I was too inebriated to defend myself, I probably would have a drink in my hand now. I was sure other people had a different version of rock bottom, but mine was staring death straight in the face.

"That's incredible!" Dennison said.

I could hear the smile in his voice. I glanced across the living room to my mantel, where a framed photograph shone even in the dimness of the apartment. It was the day I graduated from the academy, and Dennison stood by my side. His dark skin contrasted against my freckled pallor, and both of us grinned as wide as the sky.

"Thanks, it's been tough, but I'm getting through it."

I thought about mentioning the letter I received about Zac, but Dennison cleared his throat and continued speaking, "Listen, I was actually calling on a bit of business."

"Yeah?" I chewed on the inside of my cheek while Salem purred at my feet. I closed my eyes and waited for Dennison to tell me they could no longer keep me on the payroll and administrative leave. My thoughts skyrocketed to what I'd do next. Did I even have a resume prepared? Who would hire me? Could I afford to keep my cozy apartment?

"We need you to come back, Dahlia."

"What?" I turned in my spot on the windowsill, much to Salem's dismay. "You're not letting me go?"

Dennison chuckled. "Not yet. We've had a few promotions and a few transfers. The department is as thin as it's ever been. We're all working overtime, and it's showing, if you know what I mean."

Of course I knew. Overworked detectives could easily lead to lazy detectives, or at the very least, ones who missed the smallest yet most crucial detail in cracking a case. I'd already been cleared by the department's therapist and had a few sessions of grief counseling.

"I'll take it," I said. "I'm ready to come back."

"Well, then it's settled. Why don't you swing by tomorrow morning, and we'll start the paperwork?"

"I'll be there."

For the first time in a very long time, it seemed as though I was dealt a card in my favor. Things were looking up for me, and I couldn't wait.

TWO

The following morning, I woke up with clammy hands and a pounding heart. I couldn't believe the day had finally come: I was going back to work. Being in law enforcement defined who I was as a person. Without it, I didn't know who I'd be or what I'd do. I was sure I could find another job, something else to pass the time, but when you found your passion, your true calling, there wasn't much else that would satiate you.

Turning the faucet on, I jumped into the steamy shower and scrubbed away the lasting residue of the last few months. I wanted to not only cleanse myself mentally but physically too. I lathered my hair with my new shampoo and conditioner, appreciating every second the water showered my back.

Once I was dressed, the clock read eight in the morning. I still had an hour before I could go into the station to meet Captain Dennison and start my paperwork. What could I do until then? I paced circles across the living room while Salem eyed me suspiciously.

"I know, I'm nervous too," I said to my cat.

Salem scattered, and I figured I should do the same.

I slid on my one-inch heels to complete my outfit, which consisted of a black blazer, dress pants, and a white button-up top. I wanted to look presentable as I reentered the workforce. I was sure I'd get some of my brothers and sisters in blue laughing at the sight of me in a monkey suit, but it'd be worth it. I needed to make a perfect impression to prove to Dennison I was ready.

I'd be too early if I drove, so I decided to walk to the station to kill some time. I only lived about seven blocks away, so it wouldn't be too much of a walk, but long enough to catch my breath along the way. This was a huge step for me, and my pulse quickened at the thought of stepping through my favorite doors once more.

While I spent a good chunk of spring in Keygate, summer quickly approached us now. There was that feeling in the air, the one of electricity and promise. The gentle breeze swirled warm air around me as I passed the street vendors and others walking along the tree-lined avenue. The sun danced in the sky well above the horizon by now, and its heat kissed my cheeks.

Ashford was so much different than Keygate. If Keygate were an old soul, quiet and retired, Ashford carried a young, vivacious heart. In my area, technically considered uptown Ashford, the streets were lined with bakeries, restaurants, cafes, boutiques, small businesses, and more. We had a small grocery store, too, only a few blocks away from my apartment. I had everything I needed right here. Well, I did. Until I lost my Zac.

The letter from Tiger burned inside my pocket. I never left home without it these days. I carried it with me as a constant reminder to find the man who stole my soulmate from this earth. Maybe now that I was back to work, I'd have the resources to look into it again. You know, without a bottle of booze in my hand. With a clear mind and a hunger to bring justice, I'd hunt down Tiger and bring him a lifetime of captivity, or better, death.

Halfway to the station, I noticed a new cafe, Split Bean, opened up on the corner of 7th and Cherry Street. A hand-painted mural on the side of the building caught my eye with the pearly pastels swirling around a cartoonish map of Ashford. It seemed to be a growing trend: curated graffiti around the city.

I glanced at my watch and noted I had plenty of time to stop for coffee. With a smile on my face, I strolled into the cafe. A pretty young woman stood behind the counter with reddish curls lying loosely down her back.

"Good morning, what would you like to order?"

I scanned the chalkboard menu above the register and decided to keep it simple with an Americano.

"Coming right up! Would you like a pastry to go with your coffee?"

She'd be good in sales.

"Well, I'm trying to watch my weight," I said with a sly grin.

The redhead pointed toward the baked goods to a pastry on the top shelf. "Our whole-grain carrot cake muffin isn't too bad! And it's my favorite."

"Sold," I said.

I paid for my coffee and muffin. Standing to the side of the register while I waited for my order to be ready, I looked around the cafe. The walls were lined with the artwork of local artists; some of the names I recognized. There were a few puffy chairs and some other couches against the opposite wall. If I wasn't so excited to head back to work today, I could imagine hanging out here all day, reading books and drinking coffee.

"Americano and a muffin?" a woman behind the counter announced.

I looked over, and the woman with my order and I locked

eyes. My heart skipped a beat, and my breath caught in my throat. I wanted to scream and cry all at the same time.

"Bunny?" I whispered.

She shook her head and looked down toward her name tag: Kira.

So, that's her real name.

Pride burst through my chest. I always wanted my dear friend to get off the streets and into a safer job. Before Zac died, while she was still my C.I., I couldn't help but worry about Bunny almost every night. Sometimes, when I'd meet up with her, bruises lined her arms or circled an eye. Once, I found her in an alleyway, shaken and petrified of the man who left her there. I wanted to take her to the hospital, but she refused. She didn't have health insurance and didn't want to be stuck with an astronomical bill. She was more than just my informant; she was my friend. And, I knew our relationship was against protocol, and that I could even be fired if Dennison found out. But, it didn't matter; I cared for her more than I cared for following the rules. It was the one exception I made in the line of duty.

I wanted to hug her and tell her how sorry I was for the last time we saw each other. In a drunken rage, I exploded because she didn't have any information about Zac's killer. I wanted to blame someone, anyone, so I partially blamed her at that moment. It'd been the last time I saw her until now.

"Thank you so much," I said.

A weak smile broke across her painted lips. Her hair was no longer in a styled afro but was tastefully braided. She'd also tossed away the cheap cherry red lipstick and donned a subtle pink shade that contrasted beautifully against her warm brown skin.

"We'll talk soon," she said after she handed me the Americano and a small paper bag.

"I miss you," I mouthed to her.

She winked and returned to her other duties behind the cafe counter.

My sweet Bunny.

I didn't think I'd ever see her again, to be honest. I didn't have many friends here in Ashford. Well, I had my fellow officers as friends before I burned most of those bridges, but Bunny was one of the few people apart from Zac who I could be myself around. She didn't judge me, expect too much from me, or desert me when times got tough. Even though a good number of our rendezvous involved her providing intel to me she learned on the streets, there were so many times we met up simply as friends.

Sometimes, we'd grab a pizza at a late-night joint after one of my shifts and at the beginning of hers. We'd talk about nothing and everything. We could be in our own little world, even though we were from completely different worlds.

Me, a middle class, white detective, and she, an African American woman who grew up with little money and did whatever she could on the streets to get by, somehow made the best of friends. From anyone else's perspective, we shouldn't have been close but maybe that was why it worked so well between us. I treasured her company and couldn't be happier to see her work during the day instead of the night. And I couldn't wait to hear more about it.

But now it was time to head back out into the sunshine and make my way to the station. Something I didn't think would ever happen again.

THREE

As I walked the final block to the Ashford City Police Station, I twisted the engagement ring on my necklace. My awareness of the environment around me piqued: a woman pushing a stroller across the street while a few officers loitered on the corner chit-chatting. At this point in the town, the hustle and bustle of the shops and restaurants thinned out as the street veered toward the interstate a half dozen miles ahead.

I glanced at my watch and noticed I was still a few minutes early.

Better early than late.

I walked past the officers on the corner, most of whom I only vaguely recognized. One, with a face only his mother could love, glanced at me a second too long to *not* know who I was. He nudged the uniformed officer beside him who appeared to be a few years my senior. Their chatter hushed as I walked by, and for a moment, I felt transported back to high school, where people casually talked about you no matter if you were in earshot or not.

I couldn't imagine the stories and gossip that floated

around the station while I was gone. I couldn't blame them too much, though. Most of the department witnessed my downfall after Zac's murder. At first, they accepted my drinking as a way to cope. But, as it worsened, it wasn't easy to ignore. Anytime someone tried to talk to me about it, I'd lash out. Scream at them. Beg them to leave me alone. What I did with Lisa's husband wasn't a secret, either. Many of the females in the department weren't shy with their distrust of me after that.

I didn't leave on the best of terms, and now, here I was, returning from the shadows. I only hoped I could prove myself to them. Show them I'd changed and was ready to return to work.

As I opened the glass entryway doors, which were reflected so one could see inside, I wondered if the captain would have changed his mind by now. Maybe he came to his senses, and once I went inside, I'd be ushered straight back out. Was I foolish to think things could finally be heading in the right direction? Was it all too good to be true?

Inside the station, my heart skipped a beat as adrenaline coursed through my veins. It looked exactly the same and yet felt completely different. It felt foreign, as though I didn't once consider it my home. While I was gone, the walls were repainted with a steel gray with navy blue trim along the floor-boards. A few new televisions were hung from the ceiling in the main office area, while I also noticed new carpet had been installed. A beautifully hand-drawn map of Ashford was hung in a glass frame on the wall, another new addition.

However, once inside with eyes closed and absorbed in the noise of the ringing phones, radios, and conversations between deputies, it didn't feel so different. Part of me knew this was exactly where I belonged. It was as though a piece of the puzzle was back in place. I felt complete, even though sweat dripped down the small of my back as my chest tightened.

"Ah, there she is!" Captain Dennison said.

One of my favorite people in the world strode toward me with a manila folder in hand and a smile on his face. "Welcome back, detective."

"This doesn't quite feel real yet." I shrugged.

"Well, get used to it. We need you here."

It was a wonderful feeling to be truly needed by another—not just wanted or satisfied with your presence, but a person who actually needed you. And by the sounds of it, Ashford needed me too.

I followed Dennison toward the back of the station and to his office. Once inside, I breathed a sigh of relief. It looked just the same as the day he told me I needed to take administrative leave. At least this room hadn't changed since I'd been gone.

The captain sat in his black leather chair behind the desk and slid the manila envelope toward me. My breath caught in my chest as I opened the folder. Inside were my detective badge and a one-page form with a highlighted letter "X" at the bottom.

"Just need you to sign and say that you're agreeing to return from administrative leave." He broke out in a smile as he slid a pen my way.

My quivering hand picked up the black ballpoint instrument and signed my name shakily on the dotted line.

Dennison clapped his hands before opening the drawer beside him and pulling out something I recognized well: my department-issued Smith & Wesson. My heart skipped a beat as he handed it to me, the chamber pointing toward himself.

"Happy to have you back, Dahlia."

My lips parted as I cleared my throat. "Me too, sir. Thank you so much."

The sun shone brightly through the shades of Dennison's office, reminding me that no matter how dark life could get, the sun would always come out again. It wouldn't be dark forever. I nibbled on my cuticles as Dennison continued to smile at me.

"You ready?"

"Absolutely. I'm eager to get back to work."

"We're eager to have you back." He chuckled.

"How's everything been with you?"

Dennison's smile faded, and his body tensed. "Well, not going to lie. It's been a difficult couple of months. My niece passed away. The funeral was tough."

"I'm so sorry to hear that." I placed my hand on his and squeezed.

I'd never met Hanna, but I felt like I knew her by the way the captain gushed about her. I knew she'd been sick as a child, but beat the cancer. I had no idea it returned. Then again, I couldn't imagine the captain would have called me to talk about it when I was so drowning in despair myself. Shame plopped into my belly. I should have been here. Been there for Dennison.

A crisp rap knocked on the closed door of Dennison's office.

"Come in."

An officer I didn't recognize stepped inside. "Uh, sir. There's a man here who's adamant he speaks to you."

Dennison massaged his temples. "Who is it this time?"

The officer, whose name tag read Fischer, ran his fingers through his ash-blond hair styled in a tight crew cut. I squinted to try and measure his height and assumed he was a few inches taller than me. His bright green eyes sparkled under the blinding incandescent lights of the office. I could smell his aftershave from where I sat. He must have been a newbie. After some time on the job, most cops were lucky to get to work in the morning with a clean shirt. Ashford wasn't like Keygate; the rate of crime was much higher.

"It's Adam Morrison, sir."

"Again? What does he want?"

"To talk about his wife," Fischer said.

Dennison looked at me pleadingly. "Well, Dahlia. You've got your first assignment."

"Yeah?"

My stomach clenched. "What's that?"

"Can you talk to this Morrison guy and figure out what his deal is?"

"Well, what *is* his deal?"

I returned to nibbling on my cuticles. Outside, in the main area of the station, a man's voice rose above several officers trying to calm him down. I heard him pleading to speak to Dennison, his voice choking up with every breath.

"Never mind," I said. "I'm on it."

I stood from my seat and pocketed my weapon and badge. For a moment, I'd forgotten how it felt to be without them.

I strode out of Dennison's office and toward the man presumed to be Adam Morrison. A few officers surrounded him like a hawk and tried to calm him down, much to his discomfort. Adam Morrison stood several inches taller than all of the officers on the floor. He wore his black hair short and buzzed, but he had the most mysterious blue eyes I'd ever seen. He carried himself with broad shoulders and tattoos lining his arms. He seemed like a tough guy who'd been around the block once or twice, but desolation filled his eyes. I recognized the feeling: complete and utter grief.

"Mr. Morrison? I'm Detective Dahlia. Why don't we go and sit down? Talk?"

He looked me up and down until he smirked. "*You're* a detective?"

"Yes, sir. Captain Dennison isn't available at the moment, so you're stuck with me."

He huffed but followed me regardless to an interview room typically reserved for suspects or those we wanted to question. We entered the gray, dreary room and sat across from each other at the round white table. The wooden chair squeaked as

I pushed myself closer to where a yellow spiral notebook lay. I reached for it and a pen from the cup beside it. This room didn't have the double-mirrored glass like some of our other interview rooms. Since this man was neither a suspect or person of interest, I figured this room would be fine enough.

"How can I help you?" I folded my hands across the table, unblinking.

He shifted his eyes and stared at the floor, suddenly more anxious than he appeared in front of the other men; however, his anger diminished some. "It's my wife."

"Is she hurt? In trouble?" I asked evenly.

"Well, she's dead," he spat and looked me square in the eye.

A shiver ran down my spine. A million thoughts raced through my mind like a NASCAR race on hyperspeed.

Dead?

"You people closed her case, but you didn't solve her murder."

I exhaled. "What do you mean, Mr. Morrison?"

"Sheesh, lady. You new around here or something?" He pulled out a pack of Marlboro cigarettes.

"You can't smoke in here," I said. "And, no, I'm not new. I've just been out of the office for a bit. Can you enlighten me as to what has been happening?"

Adam rolled his eyes. "Y'all said my wife committed suicide. But she didn't. No one believes me, but someone killed her. She'd never take her own life."

My heart sank for a moment, but I regained my composure. "If you'll excuse me, I'll be right back."

I strode out of the interview room with my heart thumping inside my chest. I knew grief like the back of my hand, but those I mourned were stolen from me. None of them willingly left. I could scarcely imagine how difficult it must be for family and friends to know that someone felt enough darkness around them to willingly depart. Was that why Adam thought she was murdered? Because he couldn't accept the fact his wife would commit suicide?

Thoughts swirled around my mind as I almost bumped into the man I was looking for. "Hey, Fischer."

He stood with stiffened shoulders a few inches from me before he took a step or two backward. "Yeah?"

"Can you get me the file on Morrison's wife? I'd like to take a look through it."

Fischer peered around me. "He still here?"

I nodded.

A few other officers in the vicinity poked their heads from their cubes to watch us. I wished they would stop their goddamn staring. It was like they were waiting on the sidelines to witness me spontaneously combust or something. I was anxious enough; I didn't need a dozen extra sets of eyes watching my every move.

Discreetly, I dug my nails into the palms of my hands to bring me back to earth, to focus me.

"I wouldn't do that if I were you," Fischer said.

The fresh scent of his aftershave wafted into my nose once more. He wasn't particularly handsome, but he carried a ruggedness about him. I'd bet a couple of Benjamins that he was a vet. I could tell by the distant look in his eye.

"Why's that?"

Fischer sighed. "He's a nutjob looking for trouble. Did you notice the track marks beside those jailbird tattoos?"

"What does that have to do with him wanting more information about the death of his wife?" My cheeks reddened. Why was he giving me such a hard time when all I wanted was the damn case file?

"Be my guest." Fischer strode away and returned a minute later with a rather light manila folder.

"Thanks," I replied tersely and spun on my heels. I strode

toward the wall beside the interview room's door. I leaned against it, with my left heel up on the wall.

I pieced through the file to see the typical items I expected: a transcript of the 9-1-1 call after Emilee Morrison's body was discovered washed up on the beach of Lake Chakatwook, a photo of Emilee in the morgue, the coroner's report stating that she'd committed suicide, and a few brief interview notes with Adam and a few of the family's friends. According to Adam, and confirmed by Dennison, he had an alibi. He was at work that day. A photocopy of his paystub lay in the file as well.

One friend, Melinda Lockhear, stated that Emilee recently had a miscarriage and took it harder than she expected.

Is that why she committed suicide?

Kyle Morrison, Adam's cousin, admitted their marriage was on the rocks. He said he didn't always get along with Emilee, but was sad for his cousin's loss.

"Emilee was a shady person; there's no denying that. But, damn, Adam doesn't deserve this; he's my bro. I'd do anything to help him through this."

However, as I read through the file, no other instances of mental illness appeared in the notes. The coroner's report declared there were no defensive wounds or traces of drugs or alcohol in her system, hence his decision to rule it a suicide.

However, something nagged at me: the person who knew this woman the best seemed to claim with all of his heart that his wife didn't take her own life. He seemed more than adamant that someone killed her. Was there truth to his claim?

I returned to the interview room to find Adam rolling his unlit cigarette between his fingers. He looked up expectantly.

"I'm going to do an in-depth review of the case file, but why don't talk a little more now? How's that sound?"

Adam nodded. I caught him staring at my chest, and color

rushed to my cheeks. I pulled my blazer tighter around my middle to cover up the top underneath.

"Did Emilee have any enemies? Anyone she didn't get along with?"

"Everyone loved Em. She was the life of the party, the kind of person people looked up to. She deserved someone way better than me, that's for damn sure. But she loved me no matter what."

"Well, for someone whom a lot of people liked, sometimes that means there are people out there who disliked them even more."

"My cousin Kyle didn't like her. We all went to high school together, and I think he crushed on her first. So, when we ended up together, he always had a little resentment. But he's my best friend. He'd never hurt her."

"I see that your wife recently suffered a miscarriage?"

Adam stared at his feet. "Yeah, it was the third one. She was pretty devastated." He looked up to me with fright. "But not enough to take her own life! We were thinking about adopting. She was psyched about giving that a try."

"Anyone else you can think of? Anyone who would want to do her harm?"

Adam sighed. "There's this one neighbor of ours. He gives me the creeps. Emilee said she always caught him staring at her outside."

"What's his name?" I took out a pen and opened a fresh page of a notebook on the table.

"Kevin. He's the manager at Pizza Bella, not too far from here."

I scribbled the name down. My head swirled. I didn't see Kevin's name in the case file as I skimmed through the list of possible suspects, which happened to only have one name: Adam. But Adam had an iron-clad alibi. How did they miss looking into this Kevin before? And I still wanted to interview

Kyle, who was only interviewed briefly during the initial investigation.

"You're going to find out what happened to my wife?"

I promised myself and Adam that I'd find out either way. Detective Dahlia was back.

FOUR

"Hey, Dahlia," Fischer called out as the clock struck six.

"Yeah?" I called. I kept my focus on the case file before me, sprawled out on my new desk. Another officer lived in my former cube.

"We're heading out for a few beers across the street. You comin'?"

My mouth salivated at the very word. The demons I squelched weeks ago whispered in my ear, growing louder and louder. I bit my tongue to prevent myself from crying out, "Yes! Yes!" I gathered up the file and looked up into Fischer's expecting eyes. "Thanks, but I'm meeting up with my trainer after work."

Lie.

However, it wasn't a bad idea. The cravings for booze mostly subsided since I went cold turkey. I didn't think I was a true alcoholic, but I also didn't think it'd be wise to hit the bottle again on my first day back.

"No problem. See you tomorrow."

Even though I suspected Fischer to be a few years younger than me, the lines etched across his forehead could have placed him at my age or even a year or two older. I watched as he joined the other rookie officers on their way out.

Now that I was back at work, I had more resources to look into the letter from Tiger. Should I show it to Captain Dennison? Would they reopen the investigation? Could *I* handle opening the investigation up to the department? I would take the time to think about it long and hard. Sure, it might be easier to have the department behind me, but would it be better?

Dennison marched out of his office with his briefcase and empty travel mug in tow. He smiled as he stood by my desk. "Good first day back?"

I nodded. "Yup. Just happy to be here. Even though I do miss my old desk by the window."

Dennison chuckled and shook his head. "Think of it as a fresh start. No bad juju or whatever it was you used to say."

Bad juju is right. I didn't want any of that in my life going forward. It surrounded me for too long already.

"Don't stay too late, all right? I'll see you tomorrow."

"Night," I called back as my boss headed toward the door.

Most of the day-shift officers left as the night-show cops ambled in. The night show in Ashford was always a gamble. Some nights you'd crank out all your paperwork while some were filled with call after call.

"Hey," a woman's voice said.

I jumped out of my seat, not hearing the footsteps approach. "Hey!"

Lisa stood beside me. "You coming out with us?"

I exhaled. "No, not this time. I appreciate the offer, though."

She nodded. "Well, see you tomorrow."

"See you."

Butterflies roamed inside my belly while I couldn't help but grin like a kid on Christmas. Would I finally be able to get my best friend back? Only time would tell, I supposed, but this was a good start.

My cell phone lit up beside me. I picked it up to see a text from Rami: *Still on for tonight?*

Yup, be there soon, I replied.

When I walked out of the station, the sun kissed the horizon, ready to let darkness take over. The days grew longer as spring waned and summer peeked around the corner. I couldn't wait for the warmer weather and the sweet breeze of the season.

The last time those doors closed behind me, I wasn't sure if I'd ever be back. The reality that I was finally back scared me shitless. Loving something meant there was a chance I could lose it. I shook those thoughts away. I couldn't focus on that now. One thing I learned during my time away from the station and during my recovery after Noah, my ex-boyfriend, nearly killed me was to take life day by day, moment by moment. If you started to think about everything that could go wrong, you wouldn't have the opportunity to appreciate everything that could go right.

The gym was in between my apartment and the station, so it was on my way home. I could have joined another gym across town that was mostly filled with law enforcement, but I wanted to get back on the horse without being surrounded by my brothers and sisters in blue. I didn't want them to see the uphill battle I faced trying to get back into shape.

Ashford didn't slow down for the night, not yet. In fact, it was sometimes even busier than in the mornings. Sure, commuters were on their way home, but many people, especially in light of the nicer weather, came out to walk down the strip of restaurants and shops. I missed the hustle and bustle while I was gone. Part of me yearned for the simplicity of Keygate. But even though it was my first home, it wasn't my forever home. And, that was okay.

I passed the Split Bean and wondered what Kira was doing at this very moment. I hoped to see her again soon. I couldn't put into words the elation I carried knowing she wasn't on the streets anymore. She deserved so much better, and I was thrilled she seemed to finally realize that too.

I passed a few doctors' offices, an upscale sushi restaurant, and took a left on Center Street. My fitness center, Pump It Up Athletics, glowed from the corner. Its three levels donned orange accents, and bright lights illuminated the side street. It was a newer gym to the area, and I happened to find it through a coupon in the mail.

In fact, it might have been a coupon mixed in with the letter from Tiger. A shiver shimmied down my spine as my mouth went dry. Panic hovered at the surface, but I forced it back down.

When I entered the gym, electronic music greeted me along with the familiar scent of sterile equipment and the aroma of fruit. To the left of the entrance was a counter where customers could order protein shakes, post-workout smoothies, and more. I waved at Nicole, the young woman making a smoothie, and she smiled back.

In lieu of my own, those at the gym became my family. It helped me stay on track, too, knowing I wouldn't just be going to the gym but visiting with my close friends.

"Ah, there she is. Late as usual."

I rolled my eyes as Rami stood against the wall with his muscular arms folded across his chest.

I glanced at my watch and snickered. "I'm right on time, actually. As per usual."

"Get changed and meet me by the treadmills for a quick cardio warmup."

I saluted my friend, fitness partner, and coach as I headed toward the ladies' locker room. Inside, steam and laughter filled the air. I made a quick left down the first aisle of lockers and found mine in the corner. I punched the code into the keypad, and, with a distinct bing, my locker swung open.

Less than fifteen minutes later, Rami and I ran on treadmills next to each other. He insisted we bump up the incline today and slowly work ourselves up to a higher pace. Sweat dripped down to the small of my back while Rihanna's "Only Girl in the World" blasted from the speakers overhead.

"You're trying to kill me, I swear," I panted.

"Well, if you're back at work, you need to make sure you're in the best shape of your life," he said, much less labored than I.

He was right, though. I wasn't planning on getting my job back so soon. I was sure it wouldn't be long before I was back out on the streets. I couldn't risk anything by not being at the top of my game.

After the treadmills and some minor groaning, Rami guided me toward the boxing area. This was my preferred choice of working out at the gym. It helped me take out all of my aggression on a punching bag instead of a Tom Walker bottle.

Rami, a few years older than me, used to box for a living. A career-ending concussion didn't stop him from training others at the gym. I put on my pink boxing gloves, much to the dismay of Rami, who shook his head every time he saw me wearing them.

Left, left, jab.

"Good! Now try your right hook," Rami called over the music.

As I proceeded to follow Rami's instructions, a few men lingering near the weight machines caught my eye. They were covered in tattoos, many of which I instantly recognized as symbols for the local gang, and even a few common prison designs. For a few seconds, there was a pause in between songs, and I heard the men speaking. It seemed odd they'd choose a more upscale place to work out, but to each their own.

"You think Tiger will care?" the bald one asked.

Tiger?

My heart thudded inside my chest, my pulse threatening to explode in my ears. I wanted to run over to them, ask them who they were talking about. Was their Tiger the same as my Tiger? The man I wanted to hunt down like Shere Khan?

"Hey, what's up?" Rami asked.

I couldn't pull my eyes away from the men, even though the music resumed, and I could no longer hear what they talked about.

"Who are those guys?" I asked.

Rami glanced over to them and back to me with a furrowed brow. "Why? You don't want to go messing with them."

Little did he know, that's exactly what I wanted to do.

FIVE

I took a few punches to the jaw while Rami and I finished our boxing session. I couldn't keep my eyes off the thugs who mentioned Tiger, and Rami knew it.

"Dahlia, what's up?" He wiped his brow with the bottom of his black Under Armour tank.

"Sorry, just having trouble focusing today." I shrugged.

Rami nodded to the guys now bench pressing and spotting each other. "You know them?"

"No."

He narrowed his eyes. "Really? Then why do you keep watching them out of the corner of your eye?"

"It's nothing, really," I promised.

Rami patted me on the back while other patrons passed us and filled the gym. The sun no longer filtered through the windows. Instead, the dark sky filled the glass's exterior. My stomach grumbled while I finished the last of my sports drink. I needed to get home, and I prayed for leftovers in the fridge. Without another person to cook for, it seemed kind of pointless for me to cook for one. Sure, I'd been back on track and was getting my health in order, but I still ordered out regularly. I just made sure to choose grilled chicken instead of fried, dressing on the side, you know, that kind of stuff.

"See you soon?" Rami asked.

"You got it, boss." I turned on my heels and walked toward the locker room, my jaw already turning sore from the few punches I didn't block. That'd hurt tomorrow; hopefully, it wouldn't bruise.

"Hey, Dahlia?" Rami called.

I looked over my shoulder. "Yeah?"

"Hang in there, kid." He smiled.

I couldn't help but return the favor. Rami's warm eyes and mile-long grin could thaw anyone's heart. He didn't know how much he meant to me. He picked me up when I could barely stand on my own two feet. When I couldn't run more than a ten-minute mile, he got me down to my personal best. He focused me; he reinvigorated me; he taught me that I *can* be strong. I just had to *want* to be strong.

In the locker room, I changed back into my day outfit after using an after-workout body wipe. It'd have to hold me until I could get home and shower. I rarely used the showers inside the gym. Surprisingly, I covered one too many cases about murders in a gym shower. Not here, of course, but enough to convince me to avoid them at all costs.

As I walked toward the front doors of the fitness center, I couldn't stop thinking about the guys who mentioned Tiger. They *had* to know him somehow. How many gang bangers with prison tats know a Tiger? It's not like there's a bunch of them running around Ashford. Could they be the key to unlocking the mystery of Zac's death?

I scanned the gym floor but couldn't spot them. They must have left while I changed. I sighed heavily as my heart sank. I'd have to cling to the hope I would see them here again. I waved to a few staff members before walking through the doors of the gym and into the night air.

I took a deep breath and held the warm air in my lungs. Looking up and down the street, I watched as people walked by with friends and lovers. I wondered if I'd ever be one of those people again. Would I always be alone? No one could ever replace Zac, but could I find someone else to weave their own place in my heart? Sure, going home to Salem was a treat, but my cat couldn't give me advice on a hard case. He couldn't rub my back after a difficult day or hold me until I fell asleep. Hell, Salem couldn't even run out to grab breakfast if I was too lazy on Sunday mornings.

At the corner, a few men huddled together and roared with laughter. Instantly, I zeroed in on them and noticed they were the men from the gym. The ones who mentioned Tiger!

My instincts kicked in while my skin prickled with anticipation. All rational thought went out the window as I allowed my feet to carry me closer to the men. I relaxed my shoulders and pulled out my phone, pretending to send a text, all the while keeping my attention focused on the men every few seconds.

Street lamps lined the avenue while neon marquees provided a soft glow to ebb and flow into the night, but I couldn't make out their faces any better than I could inside the gym. I racked my brains to try and recall any information from back in the day, but I was drawing a blank. Zac rarely provided details about his undercover work to keep me safe. He never broke a rule, unlike me, who was willing to bend them from time to time.

The rectangular navy blue pedestrian light turned green with the image of a figure walking, and the men walked across 7th Avenue. To the left was the police station, and to the right was home. I walked straight across the street as the light glowed with a countdown for walkers.

All rational thought went out the window. I knew it wasn't safe to follow supposed gang members at night even if I carried my gun and badge. But the other part of me longed to bring

Zac's killer to justice. I knew it was wrong to do this, and yet I couldn't stop myself. What if I never saw these guys again? What if they led me to Tiger, and I solved Zac's murder?

The Ashford PD labeled his case as an ongoing investigation, but it'd been several months now without a single lead. We didn't have the resources to only focus on his case, which shattered me to pieces. I wanted more than anything to let his soul rest, but it couldn't without justice. That's what we were all about: bringing those who wronged our city to justice.

I continued to pretend to text, all the while taking notes on my phone. There were three men, all of whom seemed to be in their mid-twenties. One was bald, and the other two had buzz cuts. I tried to recall the tattoos I remembered from watching them inside the gym. I noted everything. Sometimes the smallest details were the ones that cracked the case.

I followed them, not realizing how deep into the ghetto we ventured. My mind was filled with visions of catching Tiger and putting him away for life. I was distracted with revenge, which was dangerous. The hairs on my neck stood straight, and my mouth turned dry as my breathing quickened. All my senses turned on hyperspeed from the adrenaline rushing through my veins. I knew with each and every step my safety was less and less guaranteed.

Another block and the houses evolved into nearly decrepit buildings with overgrown grass, broken chain link fences, and dogs barking ferociously from upstairs porches. Trees lined these streets, and their overgrown branches blocked out much of the street lamps' light from hitting me. I traveled in the shadows, as did the men several yards ahead of me.

Doubt and regret crept into my mind. What was I thinking, honestly? What would I do if I approached them? Ask, "Hey, I need some info on the Tiger guy you were talking about. I think he killed my fiancé."

What would I do if I ran into Tiger out here? I didn't want

him to know I was chasing him down or following his foot soldiers.

From a house across the street, a man stood on the porch with a cigarette and wolf-whistled at me. My stomach dropped.

The men I stalked paused on a street corner, and I froze, my body turning rigid like a body in the morgue. Were they meeting Tiger? What would Tiger do if he saw me in his part of town? Would he kill me too?

Fuck! Now what?

I could walk past them, but then where would I go? I could turn around now, but then the men would be at my back. I slid my phone in my back pocket so both my hands were free. I took a deep breath to steady myself. I slowed my pace to a mere shuffle and prayed the thugs wouldn't notice me, but then again, how could they not? A woman in a bad part of town at night, all alone. It was like I carried a target on my back.

They didn't notice me yet. The men talked amongst themselves about a hundred yards away from me. Dogs barked from both sides of the street as the breeze carried a sweet aroma of marijuana down the block.

A car pulled up to the corner where the men stood. The three thugs hovered by the driver's side door and ruffled through their pockets. I swooped to my left and hid behind a tree. I knew what they were doing, and I didn't want to be caught watching.

My chest rose and fell as I licked my lips and shivers ran down my arms, causing my hair to stand on end. I pulled my engagement ring, which hung on a silver chain, from beneath my top and rubbed my fingers across it, hoping for some help from my love up in the sky.

What do I do, Zac? Should I run?

Tires screeched behind me, and I could only assume the deal was done. Their voices grew louder each second. They were walking back this way. Would they see me behind the tree?

My heart exploded as my anxiety riddled my body from the top of my head down to my toes. What would they do if they saw me? Would they hurt me? I placed my ring back down into my shirt and pulled out my cell phone.

"When's the next shipment?" one asked, his voice only several yards away.

I typed 9-1-1 into my phone in case I had to make an emergency call. Bile rose to my throat as the men's cheap cologne permeated the few feet between us.

Then, out of nowhere, someone called my name.

SIX

"Dahlia?"

In slow motion, a man walked out of the shadows from across the street. My heart stopped as my pointer finger quivered over the "Call" button on my cell phone. To my left, the three thugs I followed looked at me, then at the man striding toward me. I turned and made eye contact with the bald one, who furrowed his brows while he eyed me up and down.

"Is that you?" the man asked again. He stepped out of the shadows of the night and into the soft glow of the street lamps. As quickly as fear ricocheted within my thoughts, relief flooded over me the same way.

"Jake?" I asked, my jaw dropping.

The thugs shook their heads and whispered amongst themselves as they continued walking, not paying me another glance. I pushed off the tree trunk and flung myself into Jake's arms. Disbelief rattled my mind, but I didn't care. I was safe.

"Dahlia, what are you doing in the hood, all by yourself?"

"Better yet, what are *you* doing in Ashford?"

Jake, a good six inches taller than me, looked more handsome than I remembered. We hadn't seen each other since our college graduation, but we managed to stay in touch from time to time. Last we talked, he helped me hack into Callie Jacksun's client database, which led me to solve her murder.

His dirty blond hair no longer kissed his freckle-laden shoulders. Instead, he styled it in that messy-but-obviously-perfected kind of way. He sported a strawberry blond beard too. Butterflies fluttered inside me as he released me from his grasp.

"I was just visiting with a friend, but I've been meaning to call you," he said.

"Yeah? What about?"

"I'm going legit."

We walked back toward downtown Ashford and away from the troublesome outskirts I found myself in.

"Legit?"

"I'm done hacking, well, for a living. I'll still do it in my free time, you know? I got hired at a bank across town as head of their network security team, so instead of hacking, I'll be fighting the hackers." He chuckled.

I whistled. "Little Jake, all grown up!"

After walking a few more blocks, we finally reached the main stretch of downtown Ashford. I could see my gym across the street, while to the left was the way to my apartment.

"You never said why you were back there all by yourself," Jake said.

"It's a long story," I replied.

"Tell me over dinner?"

At that moment, my stomach grumbled, and I couldn't help but smile. "Yeah, I guess I could use some dinner."

"I've been meaning to try this new Thai place that just opened up. Wanna go?"

I nodded. "Sure, why not?"

A ten-minute Lyft ride later and we walked into Thai Me

Up. I recognized the name instantly, as I'd seen it featured in the *Ashford Times* Sunday edition. While some of the older Ashfordians weren't exactly thrilled with the name, it received rave reviews across the board.

We were greeted by a beautiful Asian woman with her long, silky black hair wrapped up with a pair of chopsticks. She sat us by a charming fountain where a stone dragon shot out water from its open mouth.

Jake ordered two waters and a pair of sake bombs for each of us, much to my whispered protests.

"What? You used to love sake bombs. Remember, we used to go to that place across the street from campus?"

Color rushed to my cheeks as perspiration pooled at the back of my neck. How could I tell Jake that not too long ago I teetered on the edge of destruction as I stared at the bottom of a bottle, or rather, several bottles?

My pulse pounded in my ears. I didn't think I'd be challenged so soon and on my first day back to work. Could I handle a drink? Should I resist? Would it be better to be honest with Jake?

"Dahlia? You okay? You look like you've seen a ghost."

I exhaled. "I just need some fresh air. I'll be back."

As I excused myself, I allowed my feet to carry me outside, where a cooler breeze rippled through my blonde tendrils.

You got this, Dahlia. You can handle it.

I gazed up into the sky, and for a moment, wished I was back in Keygate. The stars shone brighter there, without as much light pollution as in Ashford. I counted to ten and focused on breathing steadily.

I rubbed my engagement ring for strength before re-entering the restaurant. Part of me wanted to take the sake bomb and ask for another. The other part of me wished I didn't have to struggle with a simple decision.

Jake stood as I returned to my seat. Both of our drinks had

disappeared. I opened my mouth in confusion, but Jake waved me away.

"It's okay. I'm sorry I didn't realize sooner."

"Realize what?" I croaked.

"I saw the same look on my dad's face every time we went out for dinner," Jake admitted, blushing.

He didn't need to explain further; I already knew Jake's father was a recovering alcoholic. Of course, he would have understood my struggles. I was too busy wondering if he'd judge me to stop and remember he would accept me no matter what.

I cleared my throat. "So, why Ashford? It's not exactly a go-to city, especially since you were closer to New York."

It was Jake's turn to blush. "The recruiter at the bank actually found me. I never planned on relocating out here, but here I am."

My mouth turned dry as images of Jake and me in college swirled in my mind like it was yesterday. I met Jake before I met Zac and believed, had I not met Zac, Jake and I would be together today. But, as fate would have it, it didn't work out that way.

However, both of us were single and now living in the same city. Would this be our time for a second chance? Guilt flooded my body at the very thought of moving on. I knew Zac would be pissed as he watched over me with the Big Guy if I *didn't* try and move on, but how could I? It wouldn't be fair to Jake either, as I planned to dedicate my life to finding Zac's killer. I wouldn't rest until I found him, that was for damn sure.

"Last time we talked, you didn't seem to know about—"

He cut me off. "I know. I felt like such a jackass."

While Jake helped me with the investigation into Callie Jacksun's murder, and I asked him to help use his hacking skills for the good of mankind, he made a few comments about me questioning Zac's fidelity, obviously not knowing Zac couldn't cheat because he was dead.

I waved him away. "It's okay. You didn't know."

A few minutes later, our dinners arrived. I salivated as I placed the napkin in my lap and unwrapped the chopsticks beside my water with lemon.

"So, you never told me exactly why you were in that part of town." I swallowed a bite of Pad Thai, curious as to how Jake would answer.

"You first," he said with a smirk.

"Official police business," I countered.

Jake chuckled. "How convenient."

I shrugged and batted my eyelashes. Jake and I stared into each other's eyes as my stomach somersaulted. I was sure he could hear my heart pounding through my chest. It felt as though we were transported back in time, still young and full of life. We were still youngish, but we'd never be as we were when we first met. Time changed people—and not always for the better.

"You're going to laugh at me," he said as he broke eye contact with me.

"Make fun of you?" I mused. "What? It's not like you were out there trying to score a dime bag or something."

Jake's cheeks turned as red as the sweet and sour sauce beside his sushi. I nearly choked on my water as I forced myself to swallow. I burst into laughter despite the patrons on either side of us shooting daggers in my direction.

"Seriously, Jake?"

"Shhhhhh!" he hissed. "You want the whole world to know?"

I put my hands up in surrender, but couldn't calm down until a few minutes later as we finished our meals. The waitress graciously brought over a few boxes and the check.

"Well, do you wanna pay since you're such a baller?" I smirked.

"Very funny, Dahlia," Jake said as he left two twenty-dollar bills on the table. "A real comedian."

We left Thai Me Up, still in a fit of giggles. I knew Jake smoked pot back in college, but always assumed it was something people grew out of. I mean, I couldn't lie, I smoked a few joints in my day, but couldn't imagine doing so now.

"Don't you have a drug test or something at work?"

Jake shook his head. "What, are you going to arrest me now?"

"Maybe I will," I said.

As soon as the words left my lips, I instantly regretted them. Was I flirting? Did I mean to say that? It was my turn for my cheeks to turn florid. I wanted to apologize, but as I opened my mouth, words wouldn't come out. My voice betrayed me.

"Wow, never pictured you for that type of gal," Jake said.

"Well, on that note. Thanks for dinner." My heart caught in my throat as I turned on my heels toward my apartment.

"You want me to walk you home?"

"No thanks!" I called back.

"Can I see you again soon?" Jake asked.

I turned around to look at the man behind me. Even from several yards away, his eyes twinkled with kindness. I could see myself with him, in bed on Sundays eating pancakes, waffles, and talking about good 'ol times. But could I let myself be happy with him? Did I deserve a second chance at love? I wasn't so sure it was the best idea. The first man I fell for ended up being a murderous asshole. The second was dead. Maybe I was bad luck?

"We'll see!"

SEVEN

I curled up on my windowsill with a steaming cup of Chai tea and Salem at my feet. My laptop was propped up against my knees while I logged into the station's cloud database so I could virtually browse through Emilee Morrison's file.

As I entered my login credentials, I held my breath, waiting for my access to be denied. Maybe returning to work was a dream, and I'd finally woken up. Surely they couldn't have brought me back yet after all the damage I caused to my career. But before I had the chance to allow further doubts to creep into my mind, a tiny ding indicated the database accepted my credentials, and I was in.

I navigated toward the case file, which I pulled up with ease. I scrolled through, revisiting the documents I scanned earlier in the day. I mentally recalled the facts I knew so far: Emilee's husband claimed wife wouldn't commit suicide; police findings indicated she *did*. So, why would the husband be so adamant to claim the police were wrong? Was he still in denial over losing the love of his life? Hell, I knew all about that.

Or did the police miss something? It was possible. We weren't perfect, and sometimes it was a needle in a haystack that solved the case. But, if you couldn't find the needle, you had to work with what you had.

If Emilee had been murdered like the husband said, then who killed her?

First, I dug into Emilee's phone records and skimmed the subpoena ordered to obtain them. I scrolled through the pages and pages of her call and text logs. She talked to a *lot* of people, but there were two numbers that showed up the most. She spent many of her talking hours later at night, which seemed odd. Several calls to one phone number were made after midnight. I shifted in my spot, which caused Salem to leap from the windowsill and sulk away.

"Sorry, buddy," I said as I sipped my lukewarm tea.

Next, I scanned through the images of the scene and of Emilee's body when found. Her skin appeared blue as ice, which contrasted wildly against her black, silky hair. She wore a cross necklace and a blue argyle sweater. My breath caught in my throat as I realized how many pictures of dead women I'd seen in my career. Part of me was hardened to all the death, but the other part of me wanted to break down. I couldn't let myself fall, though; I had to persevere. If I cried every time a person died, I wouldn't be able to function as a detective.

Ashford PD roped off the area where Emilee was found. It was one of the few beaches in the area near Lake Chakatwook, not too far outside the city limits of Ashford. Sand dunes divided the beach between the foliage around the lake, and in the photos, dark gray clouds hung in the distant sky.

Emilee Morrison was thirty-three years old, married with no children. She was born in New York City and moved to Ashford with Adam after college to be closer to distant relatives.

Next, a scanned copy of Adam's written statement filled the screen:

My wife did not commit suicide. She was a happy person and full of life. She's never been mentally ill. Someone murdered my baby. You can't rule this a suicide. Please find my wife's killer!

I skimmed other parts of the statement, reading more about their troubles with conception and miscarriages. As I neared my third decade, I wondered if it would ever be in the cards for me. How would I feel looking back at my life if I never had children? Sadness crept into my thoughts, but I eagerly pushed it away. I couldn't simultaneously manage my fears and insecurities when I had to look through this case file.

My instincts whispered in my ear, "Something's not right here."

I looked at the coroner's report next. Emilee's body bore no signs of a struggle or defensive wounds. Her official cause of death was drowning by suicide. Lab reports showed she died at least forty-eight hours before she was discovered, making any reports of alcohol in her system invalid. However, there were no traces of drugs in her body, no track marks, nothing found in her car abandoned at the scene to indicate she overdosed in the water.

So, no history of mental illness, but no defensive wounds. What the hell happened to Emilee?

The status of Emilee Morrison's case was officially closed and ruled a suicide, but was that the right call? I stood in a very difficult spot, not wanting to question my captain during my first week back to duty, but I also wanted justice for Emilee and her family. What if someone *did* hurt her, and they were out there, free to hurt someone else? I couldn't live with myself if I let this go and something else happened.

I logged out of the police database and set down my cold tea on the windowsill. Salem, curled in a ball by the bedroom door, mewed, signaling it was time for us both to head to bed.

"I'm coming; I'm coming."

Under the sheets, a spark of curiosity kept me awake. Salem lay at the foot of my bed. These days, I slept in the middle of the bed, not on my side, and not on Zac's side. I didn't want to feel as though someone else should be lying beside me.

It was nights like this I'd ask Zac for his opinion on Emilee's case. Should I probe deeper? Accept what the department concluded and move on to the next case that would surely be waiting for me tomorrow?

As my eyelids fluttered, my phone illuminated on the end table beside me. Groaning, I reached for my phone to see one unread text waiting for me.

Sleep tight, Dahlia. Let's get together again soon.

Oh, Jake. The sweetest man I never got a chance to fall in love with.

EIGHT

"Dahlia! Morning!"

"Hey, Captain. Can I pick your brain about something for a few?"

Captain Dennison and I were alone in the breakroom filling our mugs with piping hot mediocre coffee. While I was on administrative leave, the room was remodeled. Contractors painted the walls a burgundy blue and installed new cabinetry, along with increasing the countertop space. It was beautiful even though it hurt just a touch to know things changed around here while I was gone.

"Anything for you," he said.

When no one else was around, Dennison was like a father figure to me, but he never played favorites. And, if others were in the room, he would treat me exactly the same as he would them. But it was nice to have a dad away from home. That was why I knew I could trust him with what I was about to inquire about.

"So, I was intrigued after meeting Adam Morrison yesterday."

Dennison chuckled. "Of course you were."

I sipped my coffee and playfully sneered. "Then, I pored through some of the files last night."

"Go on."

"I'm just curious why we decided to declare it a suicide when we didn't have any evidence of Emilee displaying signs of poor mental health."

Captain set down his mug on the new countertop and massaged his temples. "This was a tough one; I'm not going to lie. But we had no evidence to indicate it *wasn't* a suicide. I'm sure you saw the autopsy. No defensive wounds, no strangulation, no injuries. We just couldn't put the time and resources into a case without any indication there was something more."

I nodded. "I totally understand, but—"

"Always a but with you, Dahlia," he said with a smile.

"But my gut says there *is* something more."

Dennison scooted over and put his arm around me. "I agree. However, it's the job we have, and we can't afford to chase a case without a lead."

I understood that. I really did.

"Well, what if I looked into it? You know, unofficially."

Dennison furrowed his brow. After a few seconds he said, "I don't see why that would be a problem as long as you're not pulling department resources away from another case."

Warmth radiated throughout my body, which was rejuvenated by giddiness. It was something I could use to get my feet wet as I transitioned back to full-time duty.

"Hey, head to the briefing room in about twenty minutes. I've got some news to share with the department," the captain said.

"News?" It was my turn to cross my arms and gaze suspiciously at the person across from me.

"It affects you directly, so make sure you're there," he said, more officially.

"Yes, sir."

I leaned against the countertop and sipped my coffee, which no amount of sugar could save. I gazed around, inhaled deeply and released. For a few moments, I closed my eyes, taking in my surroundings. I was finally back. Back to work. Back home. The only way life could be better right now would be if Zac walked through the doors.

"Uh, hello?" a man's voice said.

My eyes shot open to see a tall, muscular man standing before me. He wore a Gucci suit and sported coiffed thick black hair. He towered over me and had to be at least six-foot-three. His broad shoulders pulled the suit tighter against his biceps, but it still fit perfectly. His tanned skin and almond eyes glared at me with disdain. My heart skipped a beat at the handsome, sulky man before me.

"Yes, can I help you?"

"I'm looking for Captain Dennison. You weren't at the receptionist desk, and I need to find him for a meeting."

My jaw dropped as I stared incredulously at the man before me. "Excuse me?"

He raked his fingers through his dark hair as a puzzled look spread across his face. "What? I'm just looking for the captain. Can you help or not?"

My eyes bulged while my body turned rigid. A million things to say filled my mind, but I stood there dumbfounded.

Fischer poked his head into the breakroom. "Hey, the meeting is starting in a few minutes. You both should come in now before the captain gets pissed."

Without a second thought, the handsome stranger followed Fischer out of the breakroom, through the office area and into the conference room. I massaged my temples as I strode into the conference room as well. I chose a spot by the windowsill to lean against.

"Morning," the captain said.

"Morning, Captain," the mixed group of officers and detectives responded.

"Great, glad to know everyone is awake."

I couldn't help but stare at the man across the room. Arrogant and mighty, he stood against the opposite wall.

"I'm going to get straight to the point," Captain Dennison said. "We all know how understaffed we've been for the past few months."

My stomach turned as I noticed a few glances shoot my way. I always wondered how my absence affected the department, and I guess I had a stronger impact than I originally thought. Several people nodded, including Lisa, who rubbed the bags under her eyes.

"As you've seen, Detective Dahlia has rejoined our ranks, which will supremely help with all of our caseloads. But I've decided to take on another detective as well. Everyone, if you don't know him, you will soon enough. Please welcome Detective Cameron Hanover, who is transferring from vice as a homicide detective."

Everyone's eyes shot to the handsome man across the room. A few people clapped; another couple of guys waved. Disorientation swept over me like a tidal wave. This guy was going to be working *here*?

Then the captain's eyes shot to me, and a tingling sensation shimmied down my spine. Apprehension ebbed and flowed within me. I knew this look well. He was about to drop another bomb.

"And, while I haven't had the chance to tell everyone involved, Cameron, meet your new partner, Detective Elle Dahlia."

Now, the room turned from me to Cameron and back to me again. My cheeks turned crimson as my vision wavered for a moment. I strode toward the front of the room to meet my new partner. Cameron's eyes may have bulged more than mine.

"So, you're not the—"

"No, I'm not the receptionist," I said flatly.

"You two know each other?" Captain Dennison asked.

"No," we said simultaneously.

The room fell silent as Cameron and I stared at each other, neither one wanting to be the first one to blink. Work just got a lot more interesting.

NINE

Captain Dennison concluded the meeting as the rest of the department left the conference room and returned to work. I waited until the room emptied, and it was just me, the captain and Cameron.

"So this is my new partner?"

"Yes, effective immediately. I'm sorry I didn't get a chance to tell you personally; it's been a hectic week."

My shoulders tensed. Most of the officers I'd worked with in my career were decent people, but there was always the chance of coming across a rotten egg. And the rotten egg before me sneered like his shit didn't stink.

Captain Dennison massaged his temples. "Good luck, you two."

He strode away from me without a second glance, and I knew the conversation was over. There would be no changing it. Cameron Hanover was my new partner.

"Well, partner, shall we get to work?"

I strode over to Cameron until we were nose to nose. "One: I am not the receptionist. I am Detective Elle Dahlia, and I've been with the department for over six years. I have solved more than ninety percent of my cases, and I don't take shit from anyone. Several weeks ago, my ex-boyfriend tried to kill me, but I put him in jail. If you want to play nicely, you better respect me as a detective and not play the macho man act. Got it?"

He put his hands up defensively. "Whoa, whoa, calm down. It was an easy mistake."

I closed my eyes and counted to ten. Didn't men know by now that telling a woman to calm down was the exact opposite way of calming her down?

"Fine," I said with gritted teeth.

"Great. So, what's our first assignment, partner?"

"I actually want to head to Pizza Bella—"

"Pizza this early?"

"No, genius. There's a case I'm looking into. It was close, but the captain gave me the thumbs up to look into it some more. At least until there's another case we have to follow."

"What're the details?"

"Come on. I'll tell you on the way."

With Cameron in the passenger seat, I drove us toward Pizza Bella, only a few blocks away. I couldn't help but glance at my new partner from the corner of my eye. He could have been a model or an actor, but for some reason he chose to be a cop. Would a pretty boy have enough gumption to back up his attitude? Would he be able to cut it as a homicide detective?

"You going to tell me who we're going to talk to, or what?"

I sighed. "Right. Well, Emily Morrison, thirty-three, was found dead in Lake Chakatwook. No defensive wounds. The husband, Adam, says they'd just suffered their third miscarriage, but she had no history of mental illness. Dennison ruled it a suicide as they had no evidence to point to otherwise."

"Isn't the first rule of murder that it's always the husband?" Cameron asked.

"Yeah, you're not wrong. But Adam was at work. His alibi is rock solid."

"So, why are we going to Pizza Bella?"

I parked a few blocks away from the restaurant because the early lunchtime crowd always swarmed downtown. Outside the pizzeria, shoppers weighed down with recyclable bags paraded by with friends. A taxi cab idled at the corner. Cigarette butts were strewn about the curb despite a trash can placed next to a sapling surrounded by tulips. Horns honked in the distance; car exhaust meandered down the street, and the mouthwatering scent of garlic and freshly baked bread wafted from Pizza Bella.

"Adam says one of their neighbors watched Emilee a little too closely. We're going to talk to him. He wasn't interviewed before."

Cameron and I stepped inside the restaurant, a bell signaling our arrival. A counter riddled with takeout menus and local newspapers stood in front of us. To the right was the dining room. A young girl approached the counter wearing braces and a class ring.

"Hi, how many?"

"We're actually here to see Andrew Giovanni if he's available?" We flashed our badges.

The girl, Amanda, turned around and peered over the swinging doors to the kitchen. "Yeah, I think he's here. I'll grab him."

Amanda disappeared into the kitchen, and we stepped aside to sit on the bench by the entrance. An older man walked inside and paid for his takeout order. A party in the dining room sang "Happy Birthday" to a little redheaded girl with pigtails. She squealed with delight when their server brought over a cake with several candles. Vintage posters of Ashford lined the walls. Most were black and white, and by looking at the cars, could have been taken decades ago.

Amanda returned with a chubby man at her heels. He circumvented the counter and approached me and Cameron. When he wiped his hands on his apron, he left two flour hand-prints on the black and red smock. "Hi, I'm Andrew. You wanted to speak to me?"

"Yes. I'm Detective Dahlia, and this is Detective Hanover. Can we talk someplace more private?"

He raised an eyebrow but obliged all the same. "Of course. Why don't we go to my office?"

"Perfect."

We followed him behind the counter, through the kitchen and toward the back of the restaurant. He opened a plain wooden door with a brass sign reading "Manager." Inside, there was very little space. My bathroom may have been bigger than this office. There was one desk lamp and a few gray filing cabinets against the wall. Andrew sat in the folding chair behind his desk and placed his hands on the desk.

"So, how can I help you, detectives?"

"I was wondering if you could tell me a little about your relationship with Emilee and Adam Morrison."

"Huh. Okay, well we've been neighbors for several years now. We get together in the summer for block parties and stuff. Sometimes, they take turns hosting game night with the other couples on our street. Horrible what happened to Emilee." He shook his head, a solemn expression across his distressed face.

"Would you say you were close friends with them?" Cameron asked, cutting me off.

He exhaled while he looked up out of the corner of his eyes. "I mean, not close per se. Just neighbors, you know, if we saw each other outside, we'd wave and say hello. I think my wife, Marie, and Emilee got along best between the four of us. She's been having a tough time with Emilee's suicide."

I nodded. "Of course. Such a tragedy. Um, well, speaking

of Emilee, when was the last time you saw her before she passed?"

I opened my Notes app on my phone with my fingers, ready to type. The mood shifted in the office, and Andrew tugged at his collared shirt.

"Am I missing something? Do I need a lawyer?" He crossed his arms over his chest.

"No, of course not. This is just an informal interview. We're looking into Emilee's death and had a few questions."

"Looking into her death? But she killed herself. What is there to look into?"

I sat straight in the seat across from Andrew with my shoulders back and head held high. "There may be a possibility she didn't take her own life."

Andrew's eyes bulged. "What are you saying? Someone may have killed her?" He ran his hands through his dark chestnut curls. "That's horrible! Who would ever hurt her?"

"We're trying to find that out. So, where were you on February twentieth?" Cameron asked.

He scrunched his face and looked up. "I was working, I think. My wife called me to say she went over to the Morrison's house to hang out with Emilee, but no one was home. We found out the next day she'd died."

I noted everything Andrew said, word for word. "Do you have proof that you were here? Just for record's sake?"

"Absolutely, but aren't you supposed to have a warrant?"

"It would show great faith in the case if you were able to show us now; however, it wouldn't be a problem to get a warrant for the pizza shop. It would require the place be shut down, though, if that's what you'd prefer," I lied.

"Oh, yeah, right. Well, I don't have anything to hide."

He logged into his dated computer and pulled up his time-card for that day. He let me take a picture with my phone and then, without asking, he even tapped into the files for his security camera. With the timestamp and date in the corner, he pulled up the shots of him entering the restaurant at noon and not leaving until ten that night.

"I worked a double that day. I can send you a copy if you'd like?"

"Yes, that'd be fine." I relayed my email address to him, and he sent it right away.

Andrew seemed genuine, not a criminal mastermind. Could he have altered these videos? We'd have a forensics guy look them over just to make sure.

My heart beat inside my chest while I gripped my phone.

Blood pounded in my ears.

Thump.

Thump.

Thump.

Simultaneously, mine and Cameron's phones dinged from inside our pockets. We pulled out our phones and read the message.

Need backup at a bank robbery on 2nd and Lakeland. Interviewing all the people inside.

We stood from Andrew's desk.

"Is that all?"

"For now," Cameron said.

TEN

He trailed at my heels as we strode out of the restaurant and to my car. Unlocking the door, I eased into the driver's seat while Cameron had no choice but to get in on the passenger's side again. Tension hung heavy in the air like San Francisco fog. I turned on the radio and upped the volume. I didn't care that it was a country station; I just needed something to fill the silence between us.

Out of the corner of my eye, I caught him staring quizzically at me. I shifted in my seat as we pulled out of the parking lot and headed toward the bank indicated in our text.

We sat in awkward silence as we drove through downtown Ashford until we reached the quarantined block of the bank. I parked my car as close as I could, knowing I wouldn't have any problems with the men and women in blue already on the scene. I turned the keys out of the ignition and tucked them into my back pocket as I got out of the unmarked Charger.

With Cameron following, we strode through the crowds of people loitering outside of the police tape. We quickly flashed our badges to the officers guarding the scene. Cameron, who weaseled his way in front of me, lifted up the black and yellow tape for himself, but let it drop before I could sneak under. My nostrils flared while my cheeks reddened.

Dennison was already on the scene. It was unusual for homicide detectives to aid on a robbery, or rather, any type of case outside their area of expertise, but as the captain said, we were short-staffed.

"Hey, Captain, what do you need us to do?" I asked.

"There were at least two dozen people inside. We need help interviewing them before we can allow them to leave. There were two masked men who entered the bank. One locked the door and held the security guard at gunpoint. The other ordered the tellers to fill their bags with as much cash as possible."

The crowd behind us snapped pictures on their smartphones. Adrenaline coursed through my veins as it often did on crime scenes. Hair stood on the back of my neck while my body tingled.

"No one was hurt, and it's yet to be determined how much cash they got away with," Dennison said.

"Got it," Cameron said. "We'll go inside and start interviewing."

I sighed and succumbed to following Cameron inside the bank. Once we walked through the doors, fear and uncertainty hung heavily in the air. There were women crying and holding their children, businessmen anxiously checking their phones, and a few elderly people sitting down trying to catch their breath.

This bank, one of the oldest buildings in Ashford, was declared a historic building a few years ago. Its status protected it from a foreign company that wanted to purchase it, knock it down, and rebuild on the property.

The high ceilings nearly reminded me of a cathedral, while the painted brick walls reminded me it wasn't. If I didn't know the year, I would have assumed I stepped through a wormhole to another period. It was why everyone loved this bank. It wasn't your typical corporate financial institution with marketing posters plastered across the walls. It carried a rich history that couldn't be undone.

Fischer approached us. "Hey, we need help interviewing the women over in that corner. They are still in shock, and I wasn't getting anywhere."

"We're on it," Cameron said, answering for the both of us.

We strode toward the women. "Why don't I take the lead on this?"

Cameron stopped in his tracks and turned on his heels to look me in the eyes. "Why? Because you're a woman? You think I can't handle talking to people of the opposite sex?"

I couldn't help but burst into laughter. "Actually, that's exactly what I think. It was only, what, an hour ago you automatically assumed I was the receptionist?"

"It was an honest mistake," he said nonchalantly.

I rolled my eyes. "Let's get this over with. The faster we help with the interviews, the faster we can get out of here."

"Fine."

We approached the three women sitting in the corner. They all appeared to be about my age but had children of various ages. The one woman, with jet black hair cut in a long bob, rocked her baby in her arms.

"When can we leave?" she asked.

"Thank you for your patience. We understand this has been a difficult morning. I am Detective Dahlia, and this is my partner, Detective Hanover."

Another mother, bouncing her toddler twin boys on her knees, looked longingly at us with dark circles under her eyes. "You don't even know. We just want to go home."

I opened my mouth to reply, but Cameron beat me to the punch. "We'll make this short and sweet. My partner and I will interview you three, and then you can be on your way."

I cringed at the word partner. You can't choose your family, and you can't choose your partner. I pulled out my notepad and a mechanical pencil, ready to take notes. I interviewed the woman with the dark hair first. Cameron pulled the other two mothers a little farther away for privacy purposes.

"Again, I'm very sorry this has happened to you, but we'll get you out of here as soon we're finished here."

She nodded.

I started with the preliminary questions I needed for my report. She provided her name, address, phone number and initial account of what happened while she was in line.

"I wanted to take out some money from my checking account so I could take Brayden to the doctor's," she said.

My heart ached for the little one snoozing in her arms. I quickly pushed away the thoughts popping into my head, wondering if I'd ever have a baby in my arms.

"Then, all of a sudden, these guys in ski masks walked in, and I felt like I was in a movie or something."

"Did any of them speak? Did you notice any significant characteristics about them?"

Monica nibbled on her lips. "Only one of them spoke, and his voice was deep. But it was hard to hear with his mask on. He's the one who ordered all the tellers to fill the bags with cash."

I scribbled down every word, not wanting to miss a thing. Sometimes, even the smallest detail could crack a case wide open.

"What were they wearing besides the black ski masks?"

Monica stared off and tried to recall the terrifying memory, her hands quivering as she held her son, who snored softly in her arms. Out of the corner of my eye, I saw Cameron rubbing the back of the mother with the twin boys. He almost seemed human for a moment.

"One of them was wearing black ripped jeans. It seemed

kind of odd to me to be wearing ripped jeans during a robbery. I don't know, I just thought it was weird."

I noted her recollection about the jeans as the bank grew a little quieter behind me. Many people were being ushered out of the bank by other officers.

"Thank you. Here's my card if you remember anything else. Please don't hesitate to give me a call, okay?"

She nodded. "Thanks, detective."

Cameron finished with his two witnesses, and it appeared there were no others to be interviewed. I stalked out of the bank with my notebook in tow and headed toward my car with my new partner at my heels.

An eerie sensation crept up the length of my back. I wasn't sure if it was because of my new partner or what Monica said about the robber. Either way, I couldn't wait to get the hell out of here.

ELEVEN

In the cruiser, neither of us spoke. As I drove through downtown Ashford, noticing cars unnaturally slow down in our presence, a thruway sign ahead caught my eye.

Interstate 111

Lake Chakatwook was located off this interstate route. I looked at Cameron from the corner of my eye, and surprisingly, his eyes were closed and his breathing heavy, which seemed unnatural for the smug guy who wore a top-of-the-line suit. I tried to remind myself I didn't know what went on in his life outside of work, considering we just met. Maybe he had a newborn baby and was exhausted? Maybe he'd just recovered from the flu and still dealt with fatigue?

Either way, I wasn't going to let this opportunity pass me by. But, I *did* let the station pass us by as I drove past it and took the entrance to the interstate. I know the captain told me I could look into Emilee's murder if I wasn't putting it ahead of other cases, but there was nothing that said we *had* to get back to the station right this moment. I supposed I could check out the lake where she apparently committed suicide while Detective Douchebag napped beside me.

In less than ten minutes, I exited the interstate with Lake Chakatwook in view. It wasn't the most luxurious spot in Ashford, but it was a wonderful place to bring family in the summertime. I hadn't had the chance to come here very often since I moved from Keygate. Most of my time had been consumed with the job and spending time with Zac.

As I pulled into the drive leading toward the parking lot beside the beach, I couldn't help but wonder what our lives would have been like if either of us pursued a career outside law enforcement. Would Zac still be alive? Would we be well into planning our wedding by now? Or maybe we would have eloped, and I'd have a wedding band beside my engagement ring. Then again, part of the reason why I fell for Zac was his passion for justice and wanting to keep his community safe. If he were a teacher or a businessman, would I still have fallen for him? I'd never know.

Cameron issued a tiny snore, and I tried to contain myself. He was out like a light, which was perfect for me. I pulled the keys out of the ignition and gently unclicked my seatbelt. Every movement I took, I kept my eyes on Cameron for any signs of him waking. I opened my driver's side door and maneuvered out of the car. I didn't close the door completely in fear of waking my partner up. I wouldn't be too long, anyway.

With one last glance at Cameron snoozing in his seat, I set off toward the beach and the lake. There was one clubhouse on the border of the parking lot and beach bearing signs of severe aging. The wood paneling appeared faded and smooth from years of wind and weathering.

This was probably how Emilee came here undetected, whether she truly did kill herself or someone else was to blame, no one would have seen her. The warm breeze ruffled through my hair as the greenish-blue water from the lake glittered under the sunlight. Not a soul stood on the beach beside me. The sand, chunky and littered with sticks and stones, certainly didn't look appealing to spend the day in, but maybe some people liked it that way.

I tried to position myself in the mind of a woman about to lose her life. What would be running through her mind if she were about to commit suicide? Feelings of hopelessness? Inferiority? Despair? I understood those all too well. In the throes of my month-long bender, I probably would have greeted death with open arms. The darkest of roads led us into the depths of complete and utter isolation.

But a thought still nagged at me: Emilee, on paper, didn't seem mentally ill. Did people suddenly take their own lives out of the blue?

I couldn't place my finger on it, but my gut instincts screamed within me, telling me to look closer, go further, and not stop until I found the truth.

"What are you doing out here?"

I clutched my chest and spun around. "Holy shit, you scared me!"

Cameron's eyebrows furrowed. "Yeah, well imagine my surprise to wake up and find myself alone in a parking lot by an abandoned beach."

"Maybe you shouldn't have been sleeping on the job," I said.

Ignoring my jab, Cameron gazed out to the lake. I could see the reflection of the supple waves reflected in his sparkling eyes. I looked away.

"So, why are we here, anyway?"

"This is where Emilee died."

A couple of seagulls landed on the sand and poked around in search of any kind of sustenance. The sun disappeared behind a cloud, and a tingle traveled down my spine.

I felt her presence here. The loss of life hung heavy in the air. Even if Emilee committed suicide and no one hurt her after all, a woman still lost her life here. A husband lost his wife.

I looked over to Cameron, not wanting to feel vulnerable in his presence. I didn't want the new man on campus to see any of my weaknesses, and hell, I had a lot. I wanted to be tough, strong, and indestructible. But would holding up my walls just weaken me in the end? Wouldn't it be easier to open up to another person? Maybe he could help me?

"I can feel it too," he said.

"Feel what?"

"Emilee."

I crossed my arms across my middle. How could he read me so easily?

"Why did you come to homicide? You know, from vice?" I asked, changing the subject.

Cameron approached the incoming tide, keeping enough distance so his shiny shoes wouldn't get wet. He gazed out to the gray water with his hands inside his suit pockets.

"Needed a change of pace."

I hear that.

"Something happen in vice?" I prodded.

"Something happened, but not at work." He fell silent.

The detective in me wanted to figure it out. Learn his story. Find out who he was and what kind of person he tried to be. I looked at his hand and noticed a tan line on his ring finger. Then my mouth turned dry.

"Divorce?" I asked with apprehension. Even though I had a feeling it was something much worse.

Cameron's shoulders slackened and he stared at the sand. "My wife died."

"Shit, Hanover. I'm so sorry."

My heart stopped for a moment as the ground fell out from under my feet. Instinctively, my body reminded itself to breathe as I gulped in the warm summer air. My shoulders slumping, I battled internally whether or not to touch Cameron to comfort him. I decided not to.

"Brain cancer."

I didn't know how to respond, so I stood next to him without saying a word.

"So, yeah. That's why I came here from vice. Dennison helped me through it all."

Dennison?

"Oh, you knew him before coming here?"

"Captain Dennison and I go way back," he said.

A twinge of jealousy shot through me. Dennison never mentioned Cameron to me.

I waited for Cameron to elaborate, but he stayed quiet. He raked his fingers through his dark hair. At first, he'd seemed like an ass, but maybe he was lowering his walls just a bit for me. Maybe he wasn't so bad after all. We both knew what it was like to lose someone we loved. With that kind of bond, nothing was impossible.

"We should be getting back," I said, and Cameron nodded. I turned on my heels, and with the lake to my back, I trudged through the sand back to the car.

Once we reached the parking lot, Cameron cleared his throat. "I'm married to his niece," Cameron said. "I mean, was."

I turned around in a flash. "What?"

Cameron stared at his feet and shook his head. A glimmer of sadness washed over his body. I walked back to where he stood, shocked by his confession. Even though I never met Hanna, I knew she was married. But I guess I never bothered to find out *who* she was married to—small world.

He waved me away. "Just don't go running your mouth, okay? I don't want the department to think Dennison is playing favorites. He knew I needed a change of pace. Something different. Some distractions, so he pulled some strings, cashed in a few favors and put me here. Why he partnered me with you is still a mystery, though," he trailed off.

And the walls went back up again. Maybe we weren't so different after all.

"I won't tell. I promise."

"Good. You better not."

TWELVE

C ameron stared out of the window as we drove back to the station. His hardened features reflected in the glass.

"So, if Adam didn't kill his wife, and the pizza guy is clean, who did it?"

"Well, Adam mentioned that his cousin, Kyle, may still harbor some ill will. I guess he had a crush on her while they were all in high school. So, I'd like to talk to him again."

Dark clouds rolled into the sky, and as we drove through downtown Ashford, many restaurant workers scurried to collect the outside patio furniture. The leaves on the trees ripped apart from their branches, and flecks of rain smashed into the windshield.

"I just don't see how a woman with no history of mental health issues could kill herself."

"Sometimes, people carry darkness inside of them, but bury it so deep, no one can see it. But if your instincts say there's something else going on, you should listen to them."

If only Cameron knew how well I understood that truth.

We pulled into the station parking lot. Ominous clouds blanketed the sky, and it was only a matter of time before the storm emptied itself onto the city. Without a word, Cameron and I leaped out of the car and jogged to the front doors just as buckets of rain descended from the sky. We made it inside just in time to avoid getting soaked.

We sat at our desks while Cameron eased his broad shoulders out of his suit coat and I tossed my notebook and phone on top of mine. We filled out our reports and additional paperwork in regards to the bank robbery. The other detectives on the case relayed to us that the security system was being reset while the robbery took place, which meant there were no panic buttons available for the staff to use and no video footage of the robbery itself. I could hear the hopelessness in their voices as they spoke.

The two men had worn gloves, masks, and spoke as little as possible. Without security footage, how else would they capture them? It was times like these that it hurt to be a cop because we knew in our hearts the best chance to catch them was for it to happen again and hope for more evidence left behind. That also meant for it to happen again, more people in Ashford would be affected and possibly hurt. It was a cruel cycle.

Once five o'clock hit, most of the daytime detectives and officers headed out to make room for the night shift. Cameron didn't leave with the others, and instead finished up the paperwork from the bank. With a fresh cup of mediocre coffee and extra sugar, I sat at my desk with Emilee's file before me. I pored over her phone records again and noticed a strange pattern of text messages that only happened at night. It was to a number with a different area code, well outside Ashford.

Was it a college friend? Maybe a former colleague?

I opened my internet browser on the computer and typed in the phone number. Several results popped up within seconds promising an accurate reverse phone directory. I clicked on the second result as it promised a free reverse phone lookup. I entered the phone number and got a match straight away.

Glenn Michaelson, age 45, lives in Brevard County, Florida.

The site even provided a picture, which was useful to me, but extremely creepy.

Glenn was a handsome man with chestnut-colored hair and a beard that was turning salt and pepper. Who was he to Emilee, though? He was at least fifteen years older than her. Immediately, I opened up a new tab and searched for Glenn on Facebook. In this day and age, it was far too easy to track someone down online.

I found Glenn's profile right away. I skimmed through his photos first and noticed there were several pictures of him and another woman. Her face was never shown, but there were several pictures of them and just her on a beach. I clicked one photo with her and tried to see if the woman was tagged, but she wasn't. I continued to scan the photos in hopes there'd be the one revealing the mystery woman's face.

I found a photo of Glenn and a woman's hands intertwined. The caption read, "My sweet Emilee. How I love you so."

My jaw dropped as adrenaline surged through my veins. This couldn't be a coincidence. It was past the time for those. Not only did I find out that Emilee may have been having an affair, but I also discovered my new number one suspect.

"Hanover, come look at this."

Cameron leaned back in his swivel chair and balanced as he craned his neck to see. "What is it?"

When I waved him over, he stood from his desk and came to hover over mine. He glanced at the photo, and then his eyes bulged at the caption.

"She was having an affair?"

"Looks like it," I said.

Cameron scanned the guy's Facebook page. While he leaned over me to scroll with the computer mouse, his fragrant cologne filled my nose. Not only did the man look good, but he smelled good too.

"Glenn is married. Look." He pointed to a wedding photo that Glenn posted as a memory.

"Does the wife have a Facebook account?"

Cameron searched around but couldn't find any signs of the wife's profile. "No, I don't think so."

"Weird that he posted a picture of another woman on his Facebook," I said.

Cameron pointed to his friend list, which boasted only seventy friends. "Doesn't seem like his network is that big. Easier for him to get away with it."

I couldn't help but wonder if Adam knew his wife was cheating on him. Would that be motive to have her killed? I know he didn't do it himself, but could he have hired someone? Love was powerful enough to send someone into madness. He could have easily asked a friend, or maybe a cousin to do the dirty work for him.

THIRTEEN

That night, I camped out on my windowsill while I played with my phone. My fingers endlessly typed in Adam's number and deleted it. I wanted to know if he knew his wife was having an affair, but if he didn't, I would be the bearer of bad news. And what worse news could there be to find out your deceased wife may have cheated on you?

If someone called me and said Zac hadn't been faithful to me, I would easily slip back into the depths of darkness. There wouldn't be any question about it. To carry such grief when trying to hold on to the happy memories of that person—if they were to become tainted, could a person survive that?

As a detective, I felt obligated to pursue the lead. I needed to push away my humanity just for a moment in the chase for justice. Emilee deserved justice, even if that meant tainting her memory with Adam.

I typed in Adam's number one more time and called him. The phone rang as I held it to my ear, my breath catching in my throat.

"Hello?"

"Adam? This is Detective Dahlia."

"Hi," he said breathlessly. "What's up?"

"I was wondering if we could meet up tomorrow. There's something I need to talk to you about."

"Has there been a break in the case?"

Salem leaped onto my lap and purred as I stroked his ears. My stomach rumbled, reminding me I hadn't cooked dinner yet. My appetite disappeared once I found out about Emilee's assumed lover, and eating was the last thing on my mind, although my body didn't quite agree.

"Let's meet up tomorrow morning. The Split Bean, 8 am?"

"I'll be there," Adam said.

I paced around my living room wondering what I'd say to Adam. Did he know his wife was cheating on him? If so, why wouldn't he have told the police? Salem watched me as I made circles around the coffee table, littered with recipe books, junk mail, and the letter from Tiger.

I plopped down onto my faded gray loveseat and reread the letter for the hundredth time, Emilee's case leaving my mind. Anger bubbled to the surface of my consciousness just thinking about how some selfish soul in the world could take Zac away from me. How could anyone kill another person just for the sake of doing so?

I looked to the empty spot beside me on the couch. Zac and I used to cuddle here before we could afford another, longer couch. We'd pull up our TV trays after a long day of work and scarf our microwave dinners beside each other. When we were both working our way up the ranks of the Ashford Police Department, there were many nights we ate alone while the other was on duty. The longer we spent apart the sweeter our time together. We wouldn't have had it any other way, though. We loved each other, and we loved our jobs. It was our dedication to our careers that pushed us through the lonely times.

It only got worse when Zac went undercover for the force.

He couldn't stay here because he had to live as his new identity. He stayed in a ramshackle hotel room across town, where I wasn't allowed to visit. It was as if we weren't together at all. However, we did sneak calls and texts on a burner phone as often as we could. Our love was too strong to keep us away from each other for too long.

I still remember the day he pulled me aside at work and told me about his new assignment. At first, the officer in me was thrilled he'd been tapped for it, but then the other part of me realized we'd be apart for as long as it took to take down the Jagged Edges, the gang who terrorized the city and filled its alleyways with crimes and violent drug deals. I had faith that he'd be the one to end their reign.

He got so close too. Otherwise, they wouldn't have killed him.

My phone rang, and I jumped at the sound. I wondered if it was Adam calling me back to cancel. Did he know I was on to him? That I'd figured out Emilee was having an affair?

However, when I looked at the screen, it wasn't Adam calling; it was my mom. "Hey, Mom."

"How are you, sweetie? Haven't heard from you in a few days."

"I'm good! Just been working."

"Oh, I'm so happy you're back. You're going to do so well."

We chitchatted for a few more minutes before I lied and said I needed to finish my laundry. As much as I loved talking to my mom, I couldn't get the dark and twisted thoughts out of my mind long enough to have a normal conversation with her. And I didn't want to tell her about the grizzly case that fell at my feet. I didn't think she could bear hearing about another young woman being killed after what happened with Callie Jacksun.

Her call reminded me to call my dad soon too. I tried to check in with both my parents from time to time, and I knew

I'd have to be more conscious to set reminders now that I was back to work and busy once more.

Eventually, I went to bed. For hours, I tossed and turned. Even Salem couldn't handle my constant movement as he jumped off the bed and stalked out of the bedroom.

My dreams were plagued by visions of Zac chasing down the gang while they conspired to kill him. I watched the entire scene and screamed for Zac to watch out, but he couldn't hear me. I yelled at the top of my lungs, but my voice was silent.

At four in the morning, I couldn't force myself to endure the nightmares for the sake of a restless sleep. I glanced at my FitBit to see that my heart still raced and my sleep count for the night was nothing more than pitiful. The empty bed beside me only further reminded me that I was alone and the love of my life was still dead. His murderer walked free while Zac lay in the ground forever.

I laced up my running sneakers and pulled my hair into a messy bun, then slipped my pepper spray into my short's pocket just before I opened a can of food for Salem. At the sound of the tin opening, he scurried into the kitchen. I scratched him behind the ears and left the apartment, locking it behind me.

As I stepped out into the early morning or late night, however you wanted to view it, I relished the silence and darkness of the street. It was too late for the bar-goers to still be out but too early for the morning commute to begin.

It was as if I had the entire city to myself. The trees swayed in the breeze while the street lamps illuminated the deserted streets of downtown. It was my city, and everyone else was just living in it.

I set off on a run. My legs carried me as fast as they would go. I didn't want a warm-up; I didn't need to start slow. I wanted to push myself as hard as my body allowed. I needed to push away the voices in my head, the voices who told me I needed justice for Zac. Just for a few moments, I didn't want to be the woman in mourning or the cop who couldn't solve his case. I just wanted to be me, Elle Dahlia.

I often changed up my route as I didn't want anyone to notice my routine. Now, I chose a different street to turn, where I often went the other way. I found myself running through a more affluent section of town where the homes cost more than ten years of my salary. This was old Ashford, a neighborhood I often admired but didn't visit frequently.

I wasn't sure how long I ran, but in no time, the darkness lifted as dawn approached. Cars trickled onto the streets as more runners descended upon the neighborhoods. The feeling of having total control and dominance over the morning waned. I looked at my FitBit to see it neared six in the morning. I ran longer than I'd ever run before. It was nice to push away the frustrations in my life, even if just for a little while.

Instinctively, my legs led me back to my apartment, where I found Salem sleeping on the couch. He looked up once I entered the apartment and returned to sleep soon after. Starving, I poured myself a protein shake from the fridge and finished it in one helping. I chugged a glass of water too.

Glancing at my phone, I remembered Adam and I were meeting at the cafe at eight o'clock. However, I planned on getting there much earlier as I wanted to try and see Bunny, er...um...Kira. I longed for a friend in my life. While most days I reveled in the solace of being on my own, many others I wished I hadn't set fire to all my relationships after Zac's death.

Kira and I were tight, thick as thieves, despite me being a cop and her being a street girl. We came from completely different backgrounds and somehow managed to connect on a deeper level.

I dressed in my favorite black cropped dress pants, a white sheer tank with a gold zipper down the front, and, lastly, a black blazer to top off the ensemble. Sure, I was a detective, but that didn't mean I couldn't jazz it up too.

I left the apartment with electricity buzzing through my body. Today would be a good day. I would see my old friend and hopefully bust open Emilee's case. If only I knew what would actually happen next.

FOURTEEN

I parked outside the cafe, lucky enough to get a spot in front of the building. Nerves sent a shockwave through my body, but I was eager to see my friend. I walked inside, and Kira stood at the counter beaming.

"Well, look who it is," she said.

I raised my hand. "Guilty."

"The usual?"

"Yes, please."

The line behind me was minimal, while the cubby with mobile orders filled up before my eyes. It was necessary in this day and age to have an app or some kind of way to speed up the process for ordering. However, I didn't mind the wait as I had plenty of time to spare before Adam and I planned to meet.

Only two other tables hosted patrons, while others walked in and walked out with their to-go orders. After several minutes, the cubby emptied, and Kira walked to my table with my order in hand.

"Thank you! Do you have a few minutes to sit and chat?"

Kira raised her painted eyebrows.

"Nothing is wrong; I just miss you is all," I said in a hushed tone.

Kira smiled and took a seat across from me. "You know everyone is going to be suspicious I'm hanging out with a detective."

"Maybe they won't mess with you, then." I smirked.

"Honey, please. No one messes with me now."

My heart filled with love to be in such close proximity to my dear friend. Her wit and sass always kept me on my toes, and I couldn't be happier that she got out of the business.

"So, how's everything going? Do you like it here?"

"I do," she said. "It's different, obviously. But I'm very content."

"You have no idea how thrilled I am to see you here. You know I only wanted the best for you."

She nodded. "I know."

"Just out of curiosity, how did you get out? How did you get the job here?"

Kira looked out the window and gazed into the distance. Her voice trembled as she opened her mouth to speak. "I had a really bad John one night. He knocked me unconscious after I told him he didn't pay me enough. I woke up without any of my clothes on in an alleyway. He had a knife in his hand, said he was going to slit my throat and put in some diamond earrings for my funeral. He was going to kill me, Elle."

I reached for her hands and took them in mine. "Oh my God! I'm so, so sorry, Kira."

She pulled away and flicked a tear from her cheek before forcing a smile. "Luckily, some guys from the Jagged Edges walked by. The guy got so scared, he ran away. The guys dropped me off at the hospital. That was my wakeup call. And, well, anyway, one of my nurses knew my history and told me her husband was opening this coffee shop."

"I'm so happy everything worked out okay. You're doing well?"

"Oh yeah, girl. I even have my own place. It's just a one-bedroom studio, but it's all I need."

I sipped my Americano as the caffeine's warmth spread through my body. Smooth jazz crooned from the speakers overhead while I noticed pedestrians passing by through the corner of my eye.

"I'm sorry I wasn't here to help you." A stream of regret bubbled up to the surface. I'd promised her I would always be there for her, and then I disappeared in a haze of booze and depression.

She waved me away. "Girl, you have nothing to apologize for. I knew you were going through some shit. But I also knew you'd be back."

"You did? How?"

"Dahlia, you ever look in the mirror?" She chuckled. "You're tough as shit. If anyone could come back from that, it's you."

Color flooded to my cheeks as I looked down. I always thought I was a strong woman, but the past few months truly made me question my worth as a woman and an officer of the law. But to hear one of the toughest women I knew telling *me* I was the tough one? I knew it had to be true. Not to mention Kira wouldn't butter me up just to say so. She was always the one to tell me I had lipstick on my teeth or that I really needed to get a pedicure. She never lied, and she never went out of her way to compliment someone either. So, this meant more than she could ever know.

"What's new with you, anyhow? You back on the job?"

I nodded. "Yes, I started again this week. Sober," I emphasized.

Kira nodded and pushed her manicured fingers against her

weave to adjust the long dark locks. "That's good. You go to rehab or something?"

I couldn't help but smile. "Not exactly. Well, my ex-boyfriend tried to kill me back in my hometown, so, you know, that was my wake-up call."

"Damn, D! And I thought I'd had it rough!"

I put my hand over hers. "I really missed you, Bunn—I mean, Kira."

"I missed you too, girl."

"Maybe we can get together sometime and actually hang out?"

A flood of customers rushed into the café, and Kira stood from the table as she adjusted her apron. "You got it, chick. I have a phone now, so I'll give you a call."

Bunny hopped behind the counter in preparation for the incoming orders. I sipped my Americano and checked the time, noting that Adam should arrive any minute.

The electricity of chatting with my old friend disappeared in a flash. Instead, anxiety plagued my mind as I watched the front window for any signs of Adam. I didn't want to tell him his wife was having an affair, yet here I was.

I tapped my feet against my smooth wooden chair while I cracked each of my knuckles. I sighed, noticing Adam was late. I pulled my engagement ring necklace from underneath my shirt and played with it between my fingers. A man approached the window, and my heart leaped from my chest. The man strode by, though, and my eagerness deflated.

I checked my phone to see if I missed any calls or texts, but my screen didn't show any new notifications. As I nibbled on my lip, I wondered if I'd be late to work at this point, or if I should just call it. Maybe he didn't want to come. Maybe he forgot?

I gathered my things and stood from my chair as Adam strode into the cafe. He found me and trudged to the table.

"Hey! Sorry. I, uh, had some phone calls to make. These fuckin' creditors won't leave me alone."

Sweat pooled and dripped from his forehead, and his chest rapidly rose and fell as he sat across from me. "These doctors want us to pay the in vitro bills. Well, guess what, assholes, it didn't work! I'm not paying them a damn cent. Then, you know, the bank won't give me a break on the other bills. I mean my wife is dead, give me a freaking break."

"Do you work?" I watched while mania tore through his mind.

"I was laid off after Emilee died. They said they caught me stealing from petty cash." His lip snarled.

"Well, did you?"

He rolled his eyes. "It was only once, and I paid it back! No one gets a second chance around here, ya know?"

Actually, some people do.

"So, you wanted to meet so you could tell me something?"

Normally, I would have asked Adam if he wanted to get a coffee while we talked, but we were running late as it was. I didn't have time for that, nor did I need to stall the looming conversation any longer. I tossed aside my civilian mask and tightened my detective one.

"I have reason to believe Emilee was seeing a man down in Florida. Do you know anything about that?"

A flash of anger burst in his eyes as his jaw clenched. "So, it *was* Florida, huh?"

I narrowed my eyes. "You knew she was having an affair?"

If he did kill her, why was he so insistent about finding her murderer? Wouldn't that implicate himself?

Adam ran his fingers along his buzzed hair and leaned back against the chair. "I had my suspicions, but she never copped to it. I didn't have any proof, so I didn't think it was worth mentioning to you."

Keeping secrets from the police is not a good look.

"Well, it's no secret that in a murder investigation, the prime suspects are the husband and boyfriend."

He leaned forward with his elbows on the table. His breath reeked of whiskey. Immediately, the smell piqued my senses, and a hunger boiled deep in my stomach. The sweet smell of whiskey on the tongue shot a craving up and down my body.

"So, you're saying this guy, in Florida or whatever, could have killed her?" he asked through gritted teeth.

"It's a lead I'm going to pursue."

The line inside the cafe dwindled as I checked the time once more. I was due at work in the next ten minutes for our morning staff meeting. I couldn't be late, or else the captain would ream me out in front of the station.

"Thank you, Detective Dahlia," Adam said.

Don't thank me just yet.

FIFTEEN

At the station, our morning staff meeting didn't last long. There were no updates in the bank robbery, but we added a stronger presence to the other financial institutions in the area. The men didn't get away with much; it was confirmed they managed to scramble away with ten thousand dollars. The rest of the money was secured in the vault, which couldn't be opened without a senior manager's code. That person happened to be away getting coffee while the robbery took place.

We figured that with such a small sum, they'd either be too afraid to try again or even more determined the next time. Either way, the Ashford PD wouldn't rest until they found the men responsible.

After the staff meeting, I followed my typical routine of visiting the break room for another cup of coffee. Even though I'd had one with Kira, the lack of sleep started to get to me, and it was only ten in the morning.

As I entered the break room, Lisa leaned against the counter while a new pot of coffee brewed. Her strawberry blonde locks were pulled up into a top knot on her head. I glanced at her hand to notice her wedding ring was missing. My stomach dropped. Did she and Tom break up? I hoped to God it wasn't because of what I'd done so many months ago. After Zac's murder, and when my whirlwind of drinking started, I pulled Tom into the bathroom during drinks after work. I threw myself at him, despite his desperate pleas for me to stop. I didn't remember any of it until Lisa walked in and saw us together in a bathroom stall. Of course, she didn't see Tom pushing me off; she only saw us together, my legs wrapped around him.

I hadn't talked to Lisa after that night. In fact, I hadn't seen or heard from her until I started back at the station. She was my best friend, and now we were merely acquaintances. It was sad how life worked out that way. You met someone and developed a deeper connection than you ever thought possible. Then, as the stars aligned for the worse, your reality shifted and the friendship collapsed. Someone you always thought would be in your life disappeared as though your history meant nothing. Sure, I couldn't blame her for never wanting to see me again, but it still hurt all the same.

"Hey," I said.

She looked up, and sadness etched itself across her face. "Hi."

"Gotta love how long it takes for a pot to brew, huh?"

She rolled her eyes. "Yeah, it takes forever."

I couldn't remember a time I'd been so nervous to talk to a friend or even a colleague. I wiped my sweaty palms on the back of my pants after I set my Ashford PD mug onto the countertop.

"How's everything going with you?"

"Shitty," she replied.

I cleared my throat. "I'm sorry to hear that."

"Yeah."

Awkwardness hung in the air. Lisa clearly wasn't doing so

well, and I couldn't force her to open up about her personal life, but maybe I could ask her about work. "Get any good cases lately?"

She perked up ever so much as she sprinkled the powdered creamer into her mug. "Yeah, I'm on the bank robbery case, so that's taking up a lot of my time."

"Oh, yeah. I bet! Kinda crazy they didn't leave much evidence behind, huh?"

Lisa stepped aside so I could pour myself a mug of the freshly brewed coffee. She looked me up and down, and suddenly, I felt vulnerable in her presence. I pushed those thoughts aside and focused on pouring the coffee and not spilling, despite my shaking hands.

"Yup, but I've got some boots on the ground keeping their eyes and ears open. Someone will talk or brag, and it'll travel down the line."

I nodded and sipped from my mug, burning my upper lip on the scalding liquid. I blinked away the tears and refocused my attention on Lisa. My heart pounded inside my chest as giddiness flowed through me. I missed talking to my best friend; I only hoped this would last.

"Hey, how's your former asset? Kitty, or something?"

"Bunny! She's great, actually. Working at a new cafe a few blocks away. She's off the streets."

Lisa nodded. "Good for her."

"How about you? Got any good assets these days?"

Of course our sources and assets remained confidential, but that didn't mean we didn't talk about them from time to time. We still kept their identities a secret, just used their nick-names if we wanted to share something about one.

"I've got one really great one. He's a handful, though, and impossible to deal with at times, but he's brought me some great intel."

I remembered all the quality leads Kira brought me over

the years. I solved a good portion of my cases with her help. I couldn't imagine finding a better asset like her again. As cops, or detectives, many people didn't want to talk to us, especially if they had a sordid past—or they were afraid of being known as a snitch. But not everyone who lived a troubled life was a troubled person, and there were many who *wanted* to help the police but couldn't do it openly. That was why we protected them at all costs. They went where we couldn't and knew things we wouldn't.

"What's this guy's deal?"

"Well, he got swept up into the street life when he was really young. Absent parents and all that. But now that he's with a good woman and a dad, he's hoping to get out at some point. You know how it is: once you're in, you're in or you're dead."

I nodded.

Lisa lowered her eyes. "He was actually passed off to me. He used to be Zac's asset."

My heart skipped a beat. The mere mention of his name ripped open the scars I worked so damn hard to heal.

"Yeah?" I asked.

"Yup."

Silence blanketed the conversation. I racked my brains to try and remember any assets Zac mentioned, but I came up blank. It must have been during his time undercover. And at that point, we weren't able to communicate too much to keep his act legit.

"What's his name?" I asked, trying to break the silence.

Lisa looked up, and her gaze met mine. "His name is Tiger."

My eyes widened, my mouth agape. I clenched my fists. "What did you just say?"

Lisa furrowed her eyebrows. "My asset's name is Tiger."

At that moment, it was like a train traveling full speed

ahead crushed me under its industrial steel frame. My body froze, and I couldn't breathe. My restricted breathing made the room spin. I clutched the countertop. Did she just say what I thought she said? This couldn't be happening. Lisa's asset was the man who claimed to have killed Zac?

"Dahlia, are you okay? You look a little—"

Without warning, floating white lights filled my vision as the room before me blurred. One moment I was struggling to catch my breath, and in the next, everything turned dark.

SIXTEEN

"Elle? Elle? Are you okay?" a woman's voice shrieked.

"Give her some space. Here, get out of my way," a man's voice demanded.

Reality slipped back into my consciousness, but I wanted nothing more than to fall back into the abyss of nothingness. The sensation of cold tile against my skin alerted me to wake up. As my eyes flickered, I sensed several people crowding around me, which was the last thing I wanted after passing out in the break room.

I opened my eyes to see Cameron hovering over me with Lisa in the background chewing her nails.

"Hey, partner," Cameron said.

"What happened?" I asked, woozy.

"Well, it seems you may have passed out."

"Fuck."

Cameron looked around at the other faces in the room. "She's fine. Back to work."

Feet shuffled away from me. A wave of relief washed over me as I took in a large breath, holding the air in my lungs for a few seconds before exhaling. My vision returned, and I wanted nothing more than to get off the grimy floor. Who knew when it had last been cleaned?

"Elle—" Lisa started.

"You too," Cameron interjected. "Give her some space."

Lisa's eyes bulged as she tilted her head to the side. "Excuse me?"

"I'm her partner. I'll take care of her," Cameron said.

Something in the way he said it made me feel safe. Mostly because I knew he *would* take care of me. Even though we'd only worked together less than a week, there was something about him that projected bravery and security.

Lisa craned her neck to see me. "Elle, you let me know if you need anything, okay?"

I nodded. "Will do."

Once Lisa left the break room, but not before shooting Cameron a venomous look, he and I were alone. He pressed his two fingers against the nape of my neck to check my pulse, his skin, soft and warm against mine. I batted him away as I pulled myself up into a sitting position. "I'm fine, really."

He smirked. "Fine? You just passed out at work—onto this floor. I'm guessing you know how dirty this floor is, right?"

Cameron stood and reached his hands out for me to take them. As I did, he pulled me slowly and didn't let me go until I grasped my balance. With my two feet planted on the floor, I smoothed my outfit out.

Cameron pulled out a paper cup from the dispenser and filled it to the top with ice-cold tap water. "Here. Drink."

I didn't protest. Cameron didn't take his eyes off me. I could feel his gaze burning into me. Color rushed to my cheeks, and I held on to the counter for balance.

"What's going on?" Cameron asked.

"Nothing. I must have skipped breakfast or something." I didn't meet his eyes.

"Bullshit."

I groaned. "Listen, I'm fine. Really. Let me get back to work, okay?"

"Not a chance. Let's go for a walk."

Not in the mood to argue, I followed my partner out of the office, doing my best to ignore the looks of curiosity from my fellow men and women in blue. I wanted nothing more than to be invisible. The last thing I needed during my first week back was to be portrayed as weak. Shame etched itself into my belly. I wanted to melt away into nothingness.

Outside, a few scattered clouds graced the periwinkle sky. Downtown Ashford buzzed as cars and pedestrians filled the streets and sidewalks respectively.

Cameron and I walked side by side in silence as cars with blasting music passed us by. Just his presence next to me calmed me. I wanted to tell him everything, to not be alone in all of this, but where would I start?

"So, what's up?"

I stared at the sidewalk as we strode down the street. I couldn't meet his gaze, but I could feel it upon me once again. I nibbled on the inside of my cheek as my fingernails dug into the palms of my hands.

"I know it's hard to be vulnerable and open up. But I can see it in your eyes that something is going on."

Finally, I looked over to him. "It's not easy for me to open up," I said.

"Is it easy for anyone?"

We approached a bench beside a dog park a few blocks from the station. Cameron sat down, and I followed suit. He waited patiently for me to begin. I felt like a child standing on the edge of the diving board, terrified to take the leap for the first time. My heart pounded inside my chest as I wiped my sweaty palms against my black jeans. It was terrifying to open up to someone, to bring down your walls. Because once your boundaries are down, there's no taking it back.

"My fiancé was murdered last year."

I paused, waiting for Cameron to reply, but he sat patiently and quietly beside me.

"He was undercover for the department when things went south. Someone shot him on the street."

Cameron nodded, and I knew he understood that soul-crushing grief. The kind of grief that rips through your mind, body and spirit and leaves you with nothing but sorrow and anguish.

"I went off in a tailspin after that. Buried myself in the bottle. Naturally, it affected my work, and the captain put me on administrative leave. Soon after that, I went back to my hometown for my stepmother's funeral. When I got there, a girl I babysat in high school was found murdered."

"Holy shit," Cameron whispered. "I'd heard about all of it, but didn't realize that was your man."

"It gets worse," I promised. "Still living at the bottom of the bottle, I needed something to give me a reason to live. So, I started investigating who killed Callie."

Reliving this period in my life and telling Cameron made me realize just how much I'd endured in the past year. Part of me was in complete disbelief, but the other part of me was in awe that I'd survived.

"Keep going," Cameron said.

"Well, long story short, my ex-boyfriend was the one who killed Callie. He was having an affair with her. She wanted more; he didn't. When I found out it was him, he tried to kill me too."

"Jesus, Dahlia."

"You have no idea." I buried my face in my hands.

Cars passed us by. Being outside and away from others calmed me. I no longer felt as unstable as a compromised nuclear power plant.

"After that, I got sober and felt well enough to come back

to Ashford. But, when I did, there was a letter waiting for me. It was from the person claiming to have killed Zac."

I paused, closing my eyes and trying to take deep breaths.

"The person signed it with their name, Tiger. In the break room, Lisa and I were chatting about this or that, and we got onto the subject of one of her sources. His name is Tiger."

Cameron nodded. "So, that's why."

"Yeah," I said, looking away.

He scooted toward me. With apprehension, he put his arm around me. I noticed he held his breath, waiting for me to recoil. But I didn't. I let him console me, found solace in the warmth of his touch against mine.

"And you think it's the same Tiger who wrote you that letter?"

"Do you think there are multiple gangbangers named Tiger roaming around Ashford?"

"Probably not," Cameron said. "So, what are you going to do now?"

I nibbled on my lip and gazed at the people around us. Which of them carried the same grief as Cameron and I did? Which of them caused grief for others? Every person walking by possessed their own story, their own adventures of surviving life, love, and loss. I didn't want my story to be about yearning for justice for Zac. I wanted to *get* him justice.

"Well, I'm going to track Tiger down and ask him why the fuck he killed my fiancé."

SEVENTEEN

B ack at the station, the curious glances faded as the day droned on. I impatiently waited for Captain Dennison to return to his office so I could speak with him regarding this morning's revelation about Emilee's secret lover from Florida. It was time to officially re-open the file and find Emilee's killer.

I leaned against the captain's office door, reserving my spot to talk to him first. I'd heard others talking about a meeting with the captain and the mayor, which didn't usually last too long. John Johnson, the mayor of Ashford, was in his second term in office. He'd been the sweetheart of Ashford all throughout his life. The Harvard grad turned high school teacher, football coach, principal, then he dived headfirst into politics. He campaigned on the promise to keep our schools safe and improve the education infrastructure of the city.

The city adored him, and he was re-elected with no issue whatsoever. He worked with Dennison on after-school programs for at-risk youth at the community center downtown. The mayor was busy, though, so I knew any meeting with him wouldn't last too long.

"You alright?" Lisa asked as she approached me leaning against the captain's door.

"I'm good. Thanks for checking in on me."

"You scared the shit out of me."

I blushed and turned away. "Yeah, sorry about that."

Lisa inched closer and stood next to me. "What happened? Everything was fine, then all of a sudden it was like a light switch flicked off."

Could I trust her with intel on her top asset? Would she believe me?

"So, your guy, Tiger?"

"Yeah?" she said, drawing it out.

"He wrote me a letter and admitted to killing Zac," I said through my teeth, my nostrils flaring.

She narrowed her eyes. "What do you mean?"

I rubbed the back of my neck and cleared my throat. I pulled out my phone where I had a picture of the letter saved. I didn't want to show her the original in my purse. I pulled it up and handed my cell to Lisa. Her eyes scanned the picture, furiously reading line by line. She zoomed in on the signature line, and her mouth dropped.

"It's not possible," she said.

Frustrations mounted in my mind. Was I right to tell her about the letter? Our friendship was non-existent up until this point; was it too soon to try and gain her trust? How far would she go to protect her top source on the streets?

"Then who wrote me the letter? They hand-delivered it to me. There was no stamp, so they know where I live."

"Tiger would never have killed an officer. He's trying to help us, not hurt us."

I put my face in my hands. "I'm only going off what I know, and what I know is that someone wrote me this letter and claimed responsibility for killing Zac."

I clenched my fists after I put my phone back into my

pocket. My nails dug into my skin as color filled my cheeks. Zac's killer walked free while I was held prisoner in the confines of my mind, wanting to break free and find justice for my love.

"Elle, I'm telling you, he wouldn't do—"

Captain Dennison approached us and smiled. "Ladies."

"Hi, Cap. I need to talk to you. It's urgent."

I turned away from Lisa, not wanting to speak to her anymore. I wanted to be friends again, but not if she was willing to brush away my one solid lead.

"Sure, let's go inside my office."

I followed Dennison while he took his jacket off and unloaded his pockets with keys, his phone and some business cards onto his desk. My heart thudded inside my chest as I raked my fingers through my hair.

"What's up? You seem nervous about something."

"I wanted to talk to you about Emilee Morrison," I said.

Captain sat down, and I followed suit. He rubbed his temples and looked back at me. "Yeah?"

"I have a lead."

"A lead?"

"She was having an affair," I said with confidence.

"How do you know this?"

I cleared my throat and sat a little straighter. "I combed through her phone records and saw a number she often talked to."

"The Florida number?"

My jaw dropped. "You knew? I didn't see anything in the file."

Dennison leaned back in his chair and folded his hands across his stomach. "There was nothing to find. They were just friends."

"And he said that, did he?"

I clicked my tongue and pulled my phone out. I quickly

found my Facebook app and viewed my recent search history. Glenn was the top result, and I viewed his profile once more. I scrolled through his pictures until I found the one where he mentioned Emilee. I slid my phone across the captain's desk.

He picked it up, and his eyes bulged. "Well, well, well. He certainly didn't disclose this."

"We've gotta talk to him and officially reopen the investigation. With your approval, of course."

"You really are a good detective, Dahlia. Did I ever tell you that?"

Butterflies soared inside me. For so long, I wondered *if* I ever got my job back, would I still be any good at it? Would I ever be able to regain the prestige I once held as a detective? Or would I have slipped, lost my touch?

"Thank you, sir. It means a lot."

"Would you like to do the honors of calling Mr. Michaelson for a formal interview?"

"It would be my pleasure."

"Looks like you're taking a trip to Florida, Dahlia."

EIGHTEEN

I lay in bed around midnight and turned to the other side where Zac's impression in the mattress faded away. He'd been undercover for five weeks now, and it might as well be fifty years. I missed my man so much it hurt.

We only used our burner phones to communicate when absolutely needed. There were too many ways for his cover to be blown and I didn't want it to be because I texted him a picture of the dinner I made for one.

I scooched myself over to his side and closed my eyes, breathing in his lingering scent of Guess cologne I bought him for his birthday. I squeezed my eyes shut and imagined he was just in the other room grabbing a glass of water or bringing back a slice of pie for us to share in bed. He always accommodated my sweet teeth, no matter which time, day or night.

Instead, I was by myself in our apartment while Zac was out on the streets or living with someone else in the gang. His undercover gig had no expiration date. He'd be out there as long as it took to bring down the head of the gang terrorizing Ashford: Willy G.

As I lay on his side of the bed, a distinct chirp sounded from my nightstand. My heart skipped a beat because I knew that sound: it was the ringtone I assigned to Zac's burner phone. I leaped back to my side of the bed and reached for my second phone as if it were a lifesaver and I were drowning in deep swells of an ocean.

The text message read: That one motel. One hour.

Anyone else reading this text wouldn't have any idea what it meant, but I knew it without a second thought. Part of Zac's undercover assignment required him to get as intertwined in the gang as possible, even if that meant dealing. Many of the dealers in the gang were assigned to specific posts or places to deal. Zac was assigned to a shady hotel outside of town. We agreed if we ever needed to see each other, I'd pretend to go buy from him so no one would get suspicious.

We hadn't met up yet, but I'd been looking forward to executing our plan for some time. I missed the feeling of his skin against mine. The way he smelled after a shower and wrapping his arms around me even if he wasn't fully dried yet.

Even though it was well past midnight, I jumped out of bed with a refreshed energy. I pulled on a dark pair of jeans, a worn black hoodie, and ratty sneakers. I didn't want to look like a cop, but more like a desperate junkie waiting for her next fix. However, I did put my gun in my back pocket, hidden by my baggy hoodie. Even though I was going to meet Zac, the location wasn't ideal for a woman on her own, and it couldn't hurt to be prepared.

We knew we were breaking the rules, and Dennison would totally flip if he knew what we were doing, but we were dizzy with love and pining for each other like there was no tomorrow. And we were being smart about it. It wasn't something we'd make a regular habit.

My heart exploded inside my chest as I looked at my reflection in the bathroom mirror. I rinsed my mouth with Listerine and dabbed a squirt of perfume on my neck. Bags were lined up underneath my eyes, but I didn't care. Before long, I'd be reunited with my love, and all would be well.

I got into my car, my hand trembling as I put the keys in the ignition. My mouth turned dry as my pulse quickened. Butterflies soared through my middle as I drove across town and beyond the Ashford city limits. I entered the boonies, where the streetlights flickered and the roads hadn't been paved in years. On either side of the road were acres and acres of trees. Out here, the stars glimmered brilliantly against the black night sky. During the day, it wouldn't shock a person to see a farmer driving a tractor down the road or a buggy filled with an Amish family.

The motel where we planned to meet was called Once Upon a Sleep and was known for its rough reputation. Personally, I'd been called here more times than I could count for homicides and suicides, often overdoses.

Not wanting to bring suspicion to me, I parked a couple hundred yards away in the driveway of an abandoned house. Trees surrounded the area as if it were still a forest, but a few people decided to build a road through it and a house or two. With my hand on my gun, I jogged the rest of the way to the motel. I pulled the hood over my head, which hung low, nearly covering my eyes.

I knew I was breaking the rules, and as much as I cared about following them, the line blurred between right and wrong when it came to the love of my life. I would do anything for him, and I knew it was mutual. I knew it seemed hypocritical to enforce the law day in and day out while I was about to break so many rules myself. I pushed those thoughts away. I had only one goal in mind: seeing Zac.

I knew which room he chose as we already agreed it would always be room number seven. And, in the event seven was taken, he'd choose another room and make sure to leave a sign, like a half-empty Gatorade bottle by the door or twist the curtains a certain way. We had it all figured out.

As I slowed my pace to a light jog, I didn't see any instances of other signs outside the doors of the run-down motel. My heart thumped madly inside my chest as I heard my blood pumping in my ears. Licking my lips, I knocked eight times on room seven's door. I shifted my weight from foot to foot as I heard shuffling inside the room. In a few seconds, someone removed the chain from the door and opened it a crack, just enough for me to squeeze in.

Once inside, a figure in all black pulled me into his arms. His sweet, familiar scent permeated my airways as I couldn't help but breathe him in. Within seconds, his mouth pressed against mine as he pushed me up against the door. My hood slid down while Zac intertwined his fingers into my tangled locks. Our tongues hungrily danced together while my hands roamed his body.

He picked me up, and my legs wrapped around his waist. When he grew hard against me, I moaned out of pure desperation. I wanted him. I needed him. Apart, we were strong, but together we were indestructible.

Without a word, Zac carried me to the bed with moth-eaten blankets, then he lay me down and climbed on top of me. He shimmied my pants down as I unzipped my hoodie. My lungs exploded, but I couldn't catch my breath. Time stood still for us, and nothing else mattered. I didn't care if we were in a seedy motel. I didn't care I may not see him again for weeks, if not a month.

Zac ripped my t-shirt down the middle, exposing my bare breasts. He kissed my erect nipples while he slipped his fingers underneath my panties, vigorously exploring me while my climax built and built. I ran my fingers through his hair and pulled him closer to me so our mouths connected once more.

Our kiss masked the sounds of my moans as they escalated. He removed his fingers from inside me and ripped my panties off the same as he did with my top. He slipped inside me easily, and my entire body exploded with pleasure. I attempted to call his name, but he covered my mouth with his hand as he rhythmically fucked me harder and harder.

He whispered my name into my ear as he dove deeper inside me. Sweat glistened on his back while I dug my nails into his shoulder blades. I never wanted the moment to end and yet I wanted us to finish together and feel the enormous relief as one.

"I love you," he said.

"I love you more," I panted.

With one final thrust, we each reached climax. He took my breath away and filled my heart at the same time. He collapsed on top of me, and I couldn't have been happier.

We lay together, tangled in scratchy sheets for what felt like hours. For a little while, we drifted off to sleep together, still intertwined.

When the birds' chirping and rays of golden sunshine flooded the room, I woke up, over the moon to be in Zac's arms.

Zac moaned as he shifted and turned his head to avoid the sun in his eyes. The mustard curtains could have been older than either of us. They didn't do much to keep the light out.

"Mornin'," I said.

"Hi, baby." He pressed his lips against my forehead, and a wave of sadness washed over me. I'd have to leave soon to make it to work on time and to avoid anyone seeing me leave Zac's room. My heart shattered like a vase on concrete. I didn't want to leave him. I couldn't live without him.

"Remember the last time we were in a motel?"

Zac chuckled, his dimples creasing his cheeks. I nuzzled closer and breathed him in. He smelled of sex and faded cologne.

"You mean when you accidentally booked us a one-star hotel for Valentine's Day?"

It wasn't often we could both swing a holiday away from work, but this year we managed it. I tried to book a romantic room for us in a newly renovated hotel across town, but ended up booking one of the seediest ones in Ashford by mistake. By the time we realized the mistake, it was too late to get a room at the right spot. So, we made lemonade out of lemons and spent our last Valentine's together on a moth-eaten pull-out bed overlooking the interstate.

As we lay there, I looked into Zac's eyes and wondered how I managed to snag one of the most caring men in the world. He was the type of guy to make you homemade soup when you were sick, surprise you with flowers after a long day, or check in on your best friend after her break up and you were tied up at work.

I didn't know men like Zac existed until I met him.

"When are you coming home?" Pain reverberated in my voice.

Zac sighed. "It hasn't been too long, Elle. You know it may take a while."

I knew, but I didn't want to accept it.

"But it may not take as long as I'd originally thought."

I turned to face him, delighting in his beard he'd grown out for a more distinguished look. I stroked his cheek as my heart fluttered. "Yeah?"

"*I may have a lead on who's really behind all the drug trafficking in Ashford.*"

I stared into his eyes and waited for him to continue.

"*It might go up higher than anyone ever thought. Beyond just gangs and thugs.*"

My heart skipped a beat. "*What do you mean?*"

"*I'm not sure yet, but I'm going to find out. I think some big people are involved here, Elle. Which means I have to tread even more carefully.*"

"*Are you being safe?*"

"*Always,*" *he said.*

At that moment, I knew that Zac's undercover assignment was about to get much deadlier, but I didn't know just how much until it was too late.

NINETEEN

I pressed my desk phone to my ear as I dialed the Cocoa Beach Police Station. A soft-spoken woman answered on the second ring.

"CBPD, how can I help you?"

"Hello, my name is Detective Elle Dahlia, and I'm with the Ashford PD in New York. I'm looking to speak with one of your homicide detectives."

"Of course, ma'am. One moment."

I cringed at being called ma'am; however, I knew this was a Southern thing, and I'd have to get used to it if I were to work with these people to talk to Glenn.

"Robertson here."

"Detective Robertson, this is Detective Dahlia with the Ashford Police Department up in New York. I'm hoping you can assist me in interviewing a man possibly connected to a homicide case I'm working on."

"Who's the guy?"

"His name is Glenn Michaelson; he's—"

"You wanna talk to Glenn?" the detective asked incredulously.

I cleared my throat. "You know him?"

"Yeah, I do. He's my daughter's science teacher."

Oh, fuck.

"I can assure you Glenn's got nothing to do with any murdering, but I'd be happy to bring him in so you can interview him."

I exhaled. "Fantastic. I will fly down. Do you think you can get him in for an interview first thing Monday morning?"

"I'm on it," Detective Robertson said.

I hung up the phone and breathed a sigh of relief. Robertson seemed like a good cop, but Heaven knew I'd come across one or two bad ones. It was a part of life. Just as there were some bad cops out there, there were bad teachers, bad lawyers, bad doctors, and so on. I just hoped he wouldn't play favorites with Glenn. I couldn't afford to lose this one as it was my first solid lead since returning to work. I knew I should never put all my eggs in one basket, but I couldn't help thinking about what this would do for me if I caught Emilee's killer.

I hopped onto the internet to find a cheap flight from Ashford to Orlando. Rarely did we get to travel, and when we did, it wouldn't be first class. The cheapest ticket ended up being a red eye, getting into Orlando at three in the morning on Monday. It wasn't ideal, but it'd have to do.

I looked at the paperwork on my desk and sighed.

Better finish this up now because I'll be in Florida for the next couple of days.

THE NEXT NIGHT, I tossed on an APD ball cap, and with my black carry-on luggage in tow, I nuzzled Salem goodbye before locking the door behind me. Jake promised he would stop by while I was gone to check in on Salem, make sure he was fed and even play with him if possible. Not that Salem liked to play per se, but I hated the fact that he'd be here all alone without any company. I didn't want him to think I abandoned him.

At the curb, I waited for my Uber driver to show up. Streetlights illuminated the sidewalks on either side of me, and a warm breeze washed over my face. I checked my phone, and the Uber driver was still ten minutes away.

What the hell are you doing?

A silver Hyundai pulled up to the curb, and I did a doubletake to my phone. No, my Uber driver drove a white sedan.

I rested my hand on my gun in my back pocket and waited for the person to roll down the window. As soon as they did, I immediately let go of my weapon and breathed a sigh of relief.

"Cameron? What are you doing here?"

"I heard you were heading to Florida; thought I might take the trip too."

My jaw dropped. "You're coming too?"

"You think I'd let you chase this juicy lead all by yourself and take the credit? Hell no." He winked, then leaned across the passenger side and opened the door.

I shook my head and tried not to smile. I canceled the Uber, who was somehow now fifteen minutes away instead of ten. Gingerly, I got into Cameron's car and put my carry-on between my legs.

Cameron pulled away from the curb and drove toward the airport. By this time of night, most bars and restaurants were buzzing, and I saw people loitering outside them as we sped by.

We passed a sign indicating where to enter for airport parking, then arrived at the cheapest park-and-ride. I grasped my bag in one hand and the door handle in the other. I turned to look at Cameron, whose eyes studied me intently. I hadn't noticed what he was wearing until now: gray Nike sweatpants and a fitted black t-shirt. For a brief moment, and just a moment, my heart skipped a beat. I pushed that thought away as quickly as it arrived.

"Thanks for coming with me. Not that I couldn't handle it," I added.

"Oh yeah, you could handle it, but two sets of eyes is better than one."

Less than fifteen minutes later, we arrived at Terminal 11. Cameron managed to check my Outlook calendar for the flight details so he could travel with me. The flight wouldn't depart for another forty-five minutes. While I didn't fly too often, the one thing I loved about it was the people watching. Of course, at this time of night, there weren't as many people out and about, but enough to snag my attention and help pass the time.

There were a few men dressed in suits perusing the magazine market a few terminals away, no doubt heading to Florida for some sort of morning meeting. A college-age girl with dreadlocks and earbuds lay across a row of seats and drummed against her knees. I couldn't help but wonder where these people were going and where they came from. It was always a part of my people-watching game, to assign the strangers a story.

Then, I wondered if anyone else here happened to play the same game in their mind? And if they did, what would they say as my story? With my department ballcap on, I was sure they'd know I was some sort of law enforcement officer. Could they predict my hardships? Would they be able to imagine me losing the love of my life so young?

We boarded the plane, and it couldn't have been half full. Luckily, I had an entire row to myself; Cameron sat in the row on the other side of the aisle.

Shortly after the plane ascended into the night sky, an attractive flight attendant made her way down the aisle with a cart of beverages. I eyed up all the mini liquor bottles and individual containers of wine. A little voice inside of me urged me to order one, but I chose a ginger ale instead.

I cringed anytime I thought about those long, long weeks I abused alcohol. And while myself and the doctors at the hospital agreed it wasn't an addiction I needed treatment for, I didn't quite trust myself to have another drink yet. I didn't wake up craving booze, but from time to time, I missed the sense of freefall and temporarily letting go of my emotions. Maybe another time I would have a drink to celebrate.

I must have dozed off because the next thing I knew, the captain spoke to us from the cockpit: "Welcome to Orlando."

TWENTY

I stepped out of my cost-effective motel at eight-thirty in the morning. I used an extra layer of concealer to hide how poorly I slept. On one side of my room, the guests kept me up most of the night by either arguing or making up.

Cameron met me in front of the motel with two croissants and coffees in hand. "How did you sleep?"

I gave him a look that could kill.

"That bad?" He smirked.

"Did you not hear the people in the room between us?"

"Oh yeah. I heard them all right, but I brought ear plugs."

Damn it, why hadn't I thought of that?

Our Lyft driver spoke broken English but opened the door for me once he arrived. The Cocoa Beach Police Department was only a few miles away. I awed at the palm trees swaying in the sweet, southern breeze. Even in the air conditioning of the Mazda, perspiration pooled within my underarms, and a droplet of sweat slithered down the back of my neck. I gathered my hair and arranged it into a neat top bun on my head. I glanced at my phone's camera to see a slightly disheveled version of myself, but it was a little too late to care. The driver pulled to the curb in front of the station and waved politely to me as we stepped out of the car. As he pulled away, I promptly tipped him in the app so I wouldn't forget later.

Cameron and I entered the police station, and the familiar scent of mediocre coffee wafted through the air. We approached the receptionist, who fanned herself with a stack of papers.

"Good morning. How may I help you?" Her warm chocolate brown eyes shone brightly under the fluorescent lights above us. She couldn't have been older than me but wore a wedding ring. Instinctively, I reached for mine underneath my white cotton button-up blouse.

"Detective Dahlia and Detective Hanover here to see Detective Robertson." Cameron and I showed her our credentials, and she nodded with a smile.

"Oh, yes! He's expecting you. Let me show you to the conference room."

The receptionist stood up to reveal she was several inches shorter than me. I could see over her head. We followed her through the department and toward the back of the building. I noticed the officers' cubes were filled with vacation pictures, Disney passes and cruise ship memorabilia. We stepped into a room with closed blinds on the windows.

Inside, two men sat at the table with mile-long grins plastered across their faces. One I recognized as Glenn Michaelson, and the other I presumed to be Detective Robertson. As we entered, their faces turned solemn, and Robertson sat up a little straighter and placed folded hands on the table.

Both men stood as we entered, a gesture we weren't always accustomed to in the north.

"Detective Dahlia, Detective Hanover, I'm Detective Robertson, and this is Mr. Michaelson."

"Morning, gentlemen." My partner and I sat across from

the men. I pulled out my iPhone, which I'd use to record the conversation with Glenn.

"How was the flight?" Robertson asked jovially.

"Red-eye," I said, which was all the explanation needed for the men to nod sympathetically.

"I'd like to begin, if that's okay with you?" I looked at Glenn, and he nodded. I pressed "Record" on my phone and cleared my throat. "I want to first remind you that you are here voluntarily, and you do not want your lawyer present, is that correct?"

"Yes, ma'am."

"Thank you."

Glenn jiggled his leg under the table. "If this is about Emilee, I've already spoken to your department about it."

"You have, and we appreciate your cooperation in this matter. This *is* about Emilee Morrison as some additional information has come to light," Cameron said.

Glenn sputtered. "What do you mean, 'additional information'?"

My instincts prickled more the guiltier Glenn sounded. Why was he being so defensive? What did he have to hide, besides the affair? I honed in on him like a tiger stalking its prey. "Sir, we know you had an affair with the deceased."

His eyes bulged as Detective Robertson looked at his black polished dress shoes. Glenn looked to me and to his friend, but twitching eyes landed back on me. "That isn't true!"

I shook my head. "We have proof, sir. There's really no point in lying about it. Now, what I need from you is to tell me where you were on February twentieth."

Glenn pulled out a white and black handkerchief from his sport coat. He wiped his forehead and returned the cloth to his jacket pocket. He sighed heavily. "Will this stay between us?"

I furrowed my brow. "What do you mean?"

"I mean, will you tell my wife what I'm about to tell you?"

"It depends on what you're about to say," Cameron said coolly.

If he were about to confess to killing Emilee, then his wife would probably hear it on the news before I got a chance to speak with her.

Detective Robertson turned to Glenn. "Just tell her, Glenn. It'll make things a lot easier."

My pulse quickened as I gripped the chair underneath me. Was this it? Was he about to confess? My body tensed, and I couldn't peel my eyes away from Glenn's quivering lips.

"You're right. Emilee and I were having an affair. But we only saw each other a few times a year. It was mostly an emotional affair. Even when we did meet up, either in the Keys or near her, we never slept together. I was in love with her, but we never went that far. My wife and I, you see, we've been on the brink of divorce for years. But, we've stayed together for the kids. I never wanted her to know about Emilee. It would ruin her."

"Thank you for that information, sir. Can you please tell me where you were the day Emilee drowned?"

Glenn buried his face in his hands as sobs wracked his body. "I can't believe she's gone. I really can't."

I looked at Detective Robertson, and he shrugged before he patted his friend on the back. Cameron stood from the table and paced back and forth.

I crossed my legs and tapped my pen against the table, impatiently waiting for Glenn to continue. I checked my phone to make sure it continued to record and noticed that several minutes passed, and I wasn't any closer to a confession.

"Glenn, tell the detective where you were that day so we can clear this all up."

Glenn looked up to me with bloodshot eyes and a pathetic frown across his mouth. "I went to church to confess my sins.

About the affair. I wanted to talk to Pastor John about my transgressions."

I sighed. "And do you have proof of this appointment with Pastor John? Will he confirm this is true?"

Disappointment filled my chest. I'd seen many hardened criminals over the years and stared into the eyes of cold-blooded killers, but Glenn didn't seem the type to be able to hurt a fly. I had to follow the lead, but it seemed like a dead end.

"Yes, he will confirm. He has all guests sign a book before speaking with him."

I turned to Detective Michaelson. "Can you get me that book?"

He nodded. "I'm on it."

Michaelson left the room, presumably to call Pastor John for the guestbook.

"I did love her, you know."

I nodded. "I'm sure you did."

"They said it was a suicide, but I know she wouldn't do that. Emilee was a swimmer in high school. Did you know that? No way she would have drowned."

"I don't believe it was a suicide, either," I murmured.

"Are you going to catch the person who hurt her?" He sniffed.

I thought I was about to.

"That's the plan, sir. Now, do you know anything else about Emilee? Anything at all that will help me find out who hurt her?"

Cameron sat beside me and watched Glenn with narrowed eyes. "Well, obviously, she wasn't very happy in her marriage either."

"That's convenient," Cameron shot back.

I turned toward my partner to see him seething beside me.

"I didn't hurt her!" Glenn cried.

"We'll see," Cameron said.

"How did you two meet exactly?" I asked, changing the subject.

Glenn sighed. "When my wife and I were having a particularly difficult time, I flew to Ashford for a guys' weekend. When I was out with some friends, I met her at a bar. She was so sweet and innocent, a kindergarten teacher. Her husband was a piece of work, though. We bonded over our difficult marriages."

"Why did she stay with him if she was so unhappy?"

He shifted in his seat. "Why does anyone stay in an unhappy marriage? They think they're trapped. Not to mention the fear of blowing up their lives. She kept telling me things would get better, but I knew they wouldn't."

"Did you know they were trying to have children? That she'd had miscarriages?"

Darkness crossed Glenn's eyes. His shoulders stiffened. "Yes. I knew. I kept telling her not to, and not just because I loved her and wanted to be with her, but because I knew her husband wouldn't be able to provide for the family. He was a loser. They met in high school, and she didn't know any different. She used to call me in tears saying that he spent all their money, that they were broke and living paycheck to paycheck."

"What was he spending their money on?"

"Drugs, mostly. He had a nasty habit." Glenn gazed out the window, his eyes turning glassy with sadness.

He wiped his nose with the back of his hand. "How did you find out about the affair anyway? I thought I was so careful."

"Careful enough to lie to police upon questioning?" Cameron asked.

Glenn blushed. "I know. I know, I shouldn't have lied. But I was scared."

I stood from the table and collected my things, including

my phone. I turned off the recording, seeing as I didn't need it anymore. I wasn't about to catch a killer. I wasn't about to catch anything but a flight home.

"It was your Facebook. You really should put your profile on private."

He hiccupped. "Yeah, I should, huh?"

"We'll be in touch if anything changes, but thank you for your time, Mr. Michaelson."

"Hey, Detective Dahlia?"

I turned on my heels with my hand on the doorknob. "Yeah?"

"Catch her killer, okay?"

"That's my plan."

TWENTY-ONE

Cameron and I got a ride to the beach, not too far from the station. We carried our shoes as we walked through the sand and sat by the ocean. The southern sun showered us with warmth and light.

I chewed on my nails while Cameron gazed at the vast Atlantic.

"What's up, Dahlia? You're too quiet."

"Just thinking."

"About?"

"If I'm still cut out for the job." I shrugged.

Cameron turned to me. "What are you talking about? Of course you are."

You don't know that.

"What if I'm not?"

Cameron playfully pushed me. I nearly tipped over, but caught myself. "Hey!"

"Get your head out of your ass, Dahlia. You're one of the best."

"How do you know?" I asked.

Cameron turned to look at me with smoldering eyes. "I

know Dennison never told you about me, but he definitely told me about you."

I gulped. "What did he say?"

"Wouldn't you like to know?" Cameron teased.

"Tell me," I said.

Cameron pulled himself up off the sand, rolled up his pant legs and approached the tide. I followed suit, dipping my toes in the chilled saltwater. I waited expectantly for him to spill the tea.

"He once told me if anyone were to take his place as captain, it'd be you," Cameron said.

Me?

"You're lying."

"Why don't you believe that? Don't you believe in yourself?"

"Not all the time," I admitted.

"Well, start believing."

Cameron bent low. I wondered if he saw a shell in the water, but instead he cupped his hands and splashed me with the water.

I shrieked and kicked water back at him. Beach goers around us gawked at our charade, but I didn't care. My heart felt free, even if just for a minute. Cameron tried to splash me once more, but I dodged his advances.

After a few minutes and the realization we were soaked, we called for another ride back to our motel. Needless to say, our driver wasn't thrilled we got into his car soaking wet with our legs and feet covered in sand.

Cameron and I checked out of the mediocre motel, thankful to know the next time I lay down, it would be in my own bed. However, I wasn't too lucky when it came to rescheduling our return flights home.

All the flights were booked, so we had to settle for flying standby. The airline rep said we could fly out of Orlando as early as midnight, another red-eye, or as late as tomorrow afternoon.

Cameron and I walked around the airport. Detective Robertson emailed me a copy of the guestbook page where Glenn signed into the church. I thanked him and asked for a writing sample of Glenn's as well for comparison. He obliged and promised to send it to me as soon as possible.

I was delighted in people watching, and this airport proved more fruitful than the one back home. Mostly, there were tourists and families wearing Mickey ears. I'd never been to Disney World as a child. It didn't bother me, though. My parents did their best to take me on other trips growing up. I'd been to Canada's Wonderland a few times and local amusement parks too. As an adult, I couldn't stomach the thought of paying thousands of dollars for a trip my kids would most likely not remember.

Around five o'clock, my stomach grumbled. My hands shook as I checked the time. I hadn't eaten since the morning. Cameron and I scurried toward the food court, but noticed the lines were long and crowded. I glanced to the right and a swanky bar-restaurant with barely a handful of patrons seated at their tables came into view. I knew I'd probably regret the price tag of a meal here later, but I couldn't imagine waiting in line at Chick Fil A as bratty kids screamed and whined at their parents.

"What do you think?" I asked Cameron, pointing to the restaurant.

"You know we probably can't expense that place, right?"

"I know."

With our carry-ons in tow, we stalked toward the hostess stand, where a young blonde woman greeted us. I returned her smile and couldn't help but notice her electric blue contacts and ostentatious lashes.

"How many?" she asked.

"Two please," Cameron said.

"Right this way."

I followed her over the threshold of the restaurant, and she seated us at a high-top table near the bar. She set down a menu and the drink specials, promising the waitress would be over to get our drink orders in just a minute.

I gazed at the menu, salivating at every option available. But I decided on the cheapest option: a chicken Caesar salad.

"Hi, how are ya doing today, ma'am, sir?"

"Just fine, thank you," I said.

I didn't think I'd ever get used to being called ma'am down here. It threw me for a loop each time the title graced my ears.

"What'll you be havin' tonight?"

"A water with lemon, and can we place our food orders now?" Without waiting for her answer, I relayed my dinner order to her. Cameron followed suit.

"I'll put those right in, ma'am."

The waitress brought my water right away and Cameron's Diet Coke. She forgot the lemon but I didn't mention it. Instead, I guzzled the water until a few sips remained. I hoped the drink would satiate my appetite at least until my salad arrived.

"I sure hope that wasn't vodka."

I turned to see a man sitting a few high-top tables away from us. He grinned with sparkling teeth and eyes as green as the Everglades. His sandy-blond hair lay tousled on top of his head, and he sported a crisp, white button-up shirt with a pair of dark blue fitted jeans. His voice carried a familiar twang, and I pinned him for a Southern native. Cameron eyed him.

"It wasn't," I replied.

"Well, you still thirsty? I can get ya another drink?" He eyed me up and down as though he were undressing me with his eyes.

Pretty ballsy, I thought.

Cameron looked from me to the man, and a flash of anger appeared in his eyes. "She's fine," Cameron said through gritted teeth.

The man put his hands up, surrendering. "Sure, no problem."

My cheeks turned crimson. Was Cameron trying to defend my honor? Or was he simply cockblocking me? I smiled to myself.

Cameron gripped his soda tightly.

"You okay?" I asked.

"Yup."

In the next moment, Cameron's phone rang. He answered and frowned before he hung up and looked at me. "They have an open seat on a flight leaving right now. You should go."

My stomach grumbled. I glanced at the man a few tables away, who caught my eye. "I'm pretty starving. Why don't you take it, and I'll grab the next flight out?"

Cameron also looked over to the man, who promptly turned away. "I don't know," he trailed off.

"Go, Hanover. I'll grab the next one."

"Fine," he grumbled.

Cameron grabbed his bag and stalked off toward the terminal. He gave me one more glance before disappearing around the corner.

Once he was gone, I returned my attention to the stranger. I watched as he raised the cocktail glass to his voluptuous lips. The amber liquid disappeared down his throat, making his Adam's apple bob. Part of me wanted to stride over to the man and lick his lips, to taste the whiskey on his mouth.

I hadn't had a drink in so long, but I still craved one from time to time. Especially when a debonair stranger offered me one in an airport lounge. I felt as though I were in a cartoon: an angel on one shoulder and a devil on my other. I wanted a drink, maybe to test myself to see if I could handle it. But I knew being with a stranger probably wasn't the best time to figure it out.

He looked at me. "Can I buy you a drink now?"

"I'm just going to stick with water. But thank you."

"Long delay?"

"I'm flying standby."

"Hmm. Been there." He sipped his drink. "Mind if I join you?"

I looked up to see the man glance at my left hand. In return, I looked at his.

"I can't say I'll be much company. I'm exhausted."

"Same here. But maybe we can keep other company?"

"Sure."

The man stood, his arm muscles rippling through his shirt. My heart skipped a beat as I noticed his broad shoulders and the way his shirt hugged his abdomen just right. I almost forgot what it felt like for a man to hold me in his embrace and fuel the fire inside my belly. It's not that I didn't want to feel desired, or touched. It's that I couldn't help but feel that the moment I did so, I'd be betraying Zac. What would he think if I moved on? Would he want me to move on? Would he be disappointed? What if I wasn't ready?

However, as a fire inside me burned brighter and brighter, I wondered if that was a sign that I *was* ready to move on? I couldn't stay celibate forever.

"Alex." He extended his hand, and I shook it, the touch of his skin sending tingles from the tips of my fingers to my toes.

"Elle."

"Nice to meet you, Elle."

The waitress returned with my salad and silverware in tow. "Here you are. Can I get you anything else?"

"Nope, this looks great. Thank you!"

I dug into my salad, realizing a moment too late I probably

looked like a starving animal. I coughed on a piece of chicken, and Alex patted my back.

"Easy there. Take a breath, killer."

I gulped down the bite and burst into a fit of laughter. "Sorry, I'm so, so hungry."

Alex chuckled. "All good. Hey, you sure you don't want a drink? Next round's on me."

Between the angel and the devil, I didn't have a chance to see who would win out, because one chose for me.

"Sure, I'll have what you're having."

Alex caught the attention of the bartender, an older gentleman with a handlebar mustache, and raised two fingers. The bartender nodded and reached for a bottle on the highest shelf. Electricity coursed through my veins, and I gawked as the amber liquid rushed out of its nozzle into two glasses.

I indulged in a few more bites of my salad before the waitress cruised by in time to hand us our drinks, filled much more than halfway.

Alex handed me my drink, and we clinked glasses. "To strangers at the airport."

"To strangers."

My hand quivered as I brought the glass to my lips. Time slowed as I breathed deeply, absorbing the smoky aroma of the whiskey mere inches away from my lips. Alex watched me while I brought the glass to my mouth. My heart leaped out of my chest as I tilted the glass back. The warm alcohol kissed my tongue, washing over it and burning my throat on its way down. The familiar roar of the monster filled my ears. I set the glass on the table and took another bite of my salad; the fork shook in my grasp.

It didn't take long for the alcohol to enter my body with a smooth buzz. Colors in the bar seemed brighter and the music louder. I loved the all-encompassing feeling of love rushing through my veins.

I missed this.

So. Damn. Much.

I covered Alex's hand with mine. "Hey."

He broke into a toothy grin. "Hey."

"You're not wearing a ring."

"Neither are you." His voice, dark and velvety soft, created a new wave of shivers springing down my spine.

"Are you actually not married? Or do you just take it off when you're in airports?"

"Divorced. You?"

"Widowed."

"Oh, I'm so so—"

"I'm going to go into the women's bathroom. In two minutes, you are going to come meet me. Understood?"

His eyes bulged as his jaw dropped. I didn't wait for an answer as I excused myself and strode toward the restrooms. I didn't know what the fuck had gotten into me, but I didn't want to stop myself to question it. I needed this. I needed a man's touch. To feel desired, wanted. Maybe it was the booze, or maybe it was my psyche finally cracking. This was extremely out of character for me, and I knew it, but that didn't stop me.

I entered the bathroom as an elderly woman exited and excused herself. My pulse quickened as I chose the last stall, the handicapped stall. I splashed some cool water on my face and ran my fingers through my hair to give it some more volume. Still staring at my reflection, I reached inside my bra and adjusted myself to make my breasts pop.

A few moments later, the door opened, and someone knocked on the stall door. I opened it to see Alex standing there, his lips parted and his eyes staring straight into mine.

My hands trembled as I grasped the collar of his shirt and pulled him into the stall. We stumbled backward until he pinned me up against the wall. I panted as he nibbled on the nape of my neck, and a moan escaped my lips while he made his way to meet my mouth with his. With our arms over our heads, his fingers interlocked with mine, and his tongue entered my mouth, intertwining with my own. Fireworks erupted inside me while my knees grew weak.

I felt him grow hard against me, and I wanted nothing more than to feel him inside me. I pushed aside the realization that I was in an airport bathroom with a stranger and focused on his rough hands making his way up my shirt and cupping my breasts, his breath warm against my neck. My body ached for more. I wanted all of Alex, right now, right here. My body tingled—I hadn't been kissed like this in far too long. I bit his earlobe; it was his turn to let a moan escape his swollen lips. Our chests heaved together in sync as the eroticism of the moment clouded our vision.

Anyone could walk in at any moment. The pleasure far outweighed the risk, but the idea of getting caught made it even hotter. I thought I might explode with desire.

He started to unbutton my blouse, but he fumbled over and over. Finally, he said, "Screw it," and pulled apart my shirt with brute-like strength. Buttons flew against the walls and pinged against the floor.

I couldn't catch my breath. He pulled my brassiere aside and sucked my nipple, occasionally biting it until it stung. I didn't mind the pain. It reminded me that I was here—alive. My thoughts disappeared as my buzz strengthened.

I felt for his length, hard against his jeans. He was beautifully endowed from what I could feel through the soft material of his broken-in Levis.

I reached for his zipper, and then my phone rang, the loud tone echoing inside the bathroom.

"Fuck."

"Don't answer it," Alex said as his tongue traveled from my breasts to my navel. My knees trembled, and I feared I'd lose my balance at any moment.

I glanced at my phone and saw it was a number with a 407 area code. "Hello?" I gasped.

"Ms. Dahlia? We have another seat open on the next flight you requested."

Panting, I asked, "When is it boarding?"

"In ten minutes."

"Thank you."

Was it the same flight Cameron was on? There couldn't be two flights to the same place, right?

I pulled Alex up until we were face to face, then pressed my lips against his one more time. "I'm sorry, I have to go."

"Now?" he asked incredulously.

"It was nice to meet you."

I zipped up the light sweater I wore over my blouse and left the restroom. I tossed a few bills on the table and gulped down the rest of Alex's drink. A voice over the intercom announced boarding for the fight to Ashford.

Goodbye, Orlando.

TWENTY-TWO

As the sun set over downtown Ashford, I snuggled up with Salem on the windowsill with a hot cup of Tim Horton's coffee. The buzz from the airport whiskey was long worn off. I stared outside the window at the sky, painted with pastels. My body yearned for another drink, even though alcohol clearly clouded my inhibitions. I didn't care. I wanted wine, whiskey, hell, I'd even take Baileys in my coffee. A storm raged within me, tormenting me with flashbacks of staring at the bottom of a bottle.

I thought of my body intertwined with Alex's, a stranger, in the bathroom. I still rode the high of the reckless rendezvous. Would I have gone all the way if my phone hadn't rung? I fingered my engagement ring on my necklace as I swallowed hard and winced at the memory. My chest tightened. Could it hurt to be with another man who isn't Zac? I couldn't be alone *all* the time, right?

Salem curled at my feet as I sipped my coffee. I thought of Glenn and Emilee. I was both one step closer to solving her murder and yet still three steps behind. I'd ruled out a suspect but was then again left without any leads.

I breezed through the file and read copious interviews with Emilee's friends and coworkers. No one ever suspected her of being suicidal or even depressed. Sure, some people were better at hiding it than others, but for not one person close to her to know about a battle with mental health struggles? No. She definitely didn't do this to herself. I just had to find out who did it and make sure they never saw the light of day again.

The sun dipped well below the horizon as a knock sounded on my door. Salem bounded from my feet and retreated to the bedroom. I sighed and resigned to leaving my spot, then trotted toward my door with my "Blonde roasts do it better" coffee mug in tow.

I peered through my peephole to see Jake standing there with a box of pizza and a six-pack of beers. I slipped off the chain lock and threw open the door.

"Well, look who the cat dragged in," I teased.

"When you said you were back, I figured I'd stop by." He blushed.

Stepping aside, Jake entered my apartment. The aroma of fresh mozzarella and marinara on a garlicky crust sent my stomach rumbling for a second time today. "Pizza is my favorite!"

"I know." He handed me the box and followed me into my less-than-fancy kitchen where I set the pie down onto my black and gold marbled countertop.

"I wasn't expecting company." I pulled out two plates and dug in the drawer by the sink for some clean napkins.

"I know. Just wanted to see how Orlando went. I'm guessing it went either really well or really bad if you're back already."

My eyes bulged as I opened the box and a cloud of steam rose from the large specialty pizza. I pulled at a piece and marveled as the cheese stretched the farther I pulled away. I'd worked off the salad I ate at the airport and couldn't wait to dig in.

Jake followed suit. We sat at the stools at the island and ate our slices in silence for the next few minutes. I appreciated his patience as I dogged down another slice before regaling my time down south.

"The guy was clean. He has an alibi." I wiped the corner of my mouth with my napkin. I'd told Jake a little bit about the case when I asked him to watch over Salem while I was gone.

Jake sighed. "Yeah? Damnit. Back to square one."

"Basically."

"Anything else exciting happen down there?"

I choked on a piece of the crust. Jake patted my back and handed me the glass of water I poured him before we dug in.

"Thanks," I gasped. "Wrong pipe."

Jake turned his head to see Salem slinking toward him. A smile broke out onto his sculpted face. "Hey there, little dude. Miss me already?"

I cleaned up the plates as I watched Jake and Salem out of the corner of my eye. Jake held Salem in his arms, the cat purring against him.

I meandered into the living room and reclaimed my spot on the windowsill. Jake relaxed on the loveseat with Salem in his lap.

I stared at my bitten cuticles. Talking shop with the guys at work came easy, but socializing beyond that? Sometimes, not so much.

"This is a nice place you've got here, Dahlia," Jake said, breaking the silence.

"Thanks. It gets lonely sometimes," I said.

Jake nodded. "We don't have to talk about it if you don't want to."

I shrugged. "It's okay. Just sucks."

Jake stood from the loveseat and approached me. He waved

his hand, signaling me to give him some room to sit beside me. He pulled me into his arms, and I rested my head on his shoulder. He smelled like mint and pine. I closed my eyes and breathed him in. As much as I didn't want to move on from Zac, if there were a person I could move on with, it'd be Jake. He knew me. He understood me. He cared about me.

His eyes met his. He studied me closely, and I felt like he could read me like a book.

"I'm lonely too."

"You are?"

Jake rested his chin on my head. "Yeah. Chelsea and I broke up over two years ago now."

"Have you been dating?" I held my breath.

"A little bit. You know, here and there. But I don't want to waste my time with anyone unless I know there's a future. I'm not exactly a spring chicken."

I chuckled. "We're still young...ish."

I sat up straight and looked into Jake's eyes. He returned my gaze earnestly. I felt magnetized toward him, like a compass pining for north. Jake was a good man, and I knew I'd be happy with him. Not as happy as I was with Zac, but maybe it wasn't fair to compare the two.

My pulse pounded in my ears as we leaned in a little closer, our eyes locked. I licked my lips, my heart exploding inside my chest as he bore into my soul with his eyes. When our lips neared each other's, my eyes fluttered closed.

Then, someone knocked at the door.

TWENTY-THREE

J ake and I pulled apart as my stomach dropped.

"Someone's popular," Jake said, a disappointed look plastered across his face.

I filed to the door, still unable to catch my breath, and peeked through the viewer to find Cameron standing on the other side. I opened the door, and he greeted me with a smile. He wore sweatpants and Nike dri-fit shirt.

Jake cleared his throat as he approached us and extended his hand toward Cameron. "Hey, I'm Jake, Elle's friend."

Tepidly, Cameron shook Jake's hand with tight lips.

An awkwardness wafted into the air, hanging heavily between us like fog. I gulped, not expecting for my night to turn out this way.

"Nice to meet you," Cameron said gruffly, his chest puffed out.

"Yup, you too."

I stood between my partner and best guy friend like a pickle in the middle. Cameron stared at Jake expectantly.

"Well, I guess I'll be on my way," Jake said.

Relieved, my shoulders relaxed. "Thanks for stopping by."

I couldn't take the tension any longer. Jake grabbed his wallet from the counter and nodded before leaving the apartment. The door slammed behind him.

"What the hell is his problem?"

I shrugged.

"I was coming over to see if you needed anything."

I narrowed my eyes. "You didn't want to call? You only dropped me off a few hours ago"

"Nah." Cameron strode into the apartment like he owned the place.

Cameron plopped onto the love seat and whistled to Salem, who trotted cautiously out to meet him. When he looked at me, his smile turned flat. "You okay?"

"Not really," I said.

"Is there anything I can do to help?"

"I don't think so."

"Bummed about Glenn?"

I nodded.

"It's okay. We closed one door, but another will open."

I sat beside Cameron on the loveseat, and Salem leaped onto the floor, padding away. My partner and I sat in silence for a few minutes. I watched his eyes follow the trail of photos and degrees hung on the apartment walls.

"When are you going to tell the captain about the letter from Tiger?"

I chewed on the inside of my cheek. I hadn't thought about telling the captain about the letter yet, not until I had more evidence that this gang member was involved. What if the captain went all-in on finding Tiger and scared him away? Then I'd never put him behind bars. Not to mention, I still wanted to fully earn back his trust. I gave Dennison reason after reason not to trust me before I took my leave.

I met Cameron's gaze. "I've got to play this right. If this Tiger is responsible for hurting Zac, I need to find out low-key.

If we reopen the investigation, I don't want Tiger to get spooked. I want to find him on my own."

"I don't think that's the best way to play it."

Annoyance crept in as my body tensed. "What, are you like an expert in catching gang bangers?"

"Well, actually, yeah. I came from vice, unless you forgot already."

We stared at each other, neither one blinking.

"What do you suggest, then?"

"Have you tried looking at Zac's case files from going undercover?"

"No, I haven't yet." My heart sped up. *Why hadn't I thought of that?*

"Okay, let's do it, then."

I logged into Zac's profile on our iMac and pulled up the Finder. I'd never snooped on Zac's account before. It wasn't uncommon for undercover officers to keep records of their assignments. I assumed he took his laptop with him too, where he could remote into the desktop to update his files with new information and leads. I typed like a mad scientist, looking for a folder he might have used to save his case files. My heart pounded, and my mouth turned dry. Salem rubbed up against my leg. The majority of the apartment was in shadows, while the blue glow of the computer screen illuminated our faces.

I found a folder titled *The Zoo*. I opened it and held my breath. When I skimmed through the folder, I knew I hit the jackpot.

"That's a lot of files," Cameron said. "I'll make some coffee."

I retrieved the letter from Tiger as well. I needed all the pieces of the puzzle together. For the hundredth time, I looked at it excruciatingly close. I turned it around at every angle with narrowed eyes.

Even though I'd looked at the letter every day since I came

home, I noticed something I hadn't before. In some instances, the letter "a" was thicker, and in others, they were slanted in a completely different direction.

Whoever wrote this wanted to disguise their handwriting. Did Tiger try to trick the police by purposely disguising his penmanship? Did Tiger write this at all?

I bit my lips, unintentionally drawing blood.

I meandered across the apartment and rested my head against the window. The stars illuminated the night sky despite the light pollution from the city. I traced constellations with my mind and searched the expansive sky for the Big and Little Dippers. Before I knew it, my eyes felt heavy and fluttered open and closed.

Cameron claimed my seat at the computer and started browsing through Zac's files.

"There are so many documents," I said. "The scope of this thing must be huge."

"We'll have to comb through each one of these to see if we can find who Zac was working with inside the gang. There's gotta be a lead here somewhere."

"We?" I asked.

"We're partners, remember?"

My chest bloomed. Cameron didn't have to help, but here he was, invested.

"This is going to take a long time," I said to myself, yawning. Even with the adrenaline of finding Zac's files, the fatigue from traveling weighed heavily on me.

"Why don't you get some shut eye, and I'll start combing through these?"

I shook my head. "No way. I can manage." Another yawn escaped my lips.

Cameron snickered. "Yeah. Sure, Dahlia."

He stood from the computer desk, grasped my hand and

pulled me into the bedroom. "Get some sleep. I'll wake you if I find anything super important, okay?"

"Fine," I said.

Cameron closed the door behind me, and I was left in the darkness. In bed, I glanced at the clock. Now, with access to Zac's files on his undercover missions, I knew I was on the right path to finding his killer. One way or another.

TWENTY-FOUR

Despite exhaustion dominating my psyche, I couldn't sleep. I tossed and turned until the birds chirped. I rubbed the sleep out of my eyes and yawned, twisting and turning until my back cracked. Salem launched from the bed and stood at the door, pawing to get out.

My favorite hoodie lay draped on the back of my vanity chair. I pulled it over my head, ignoring my reflection. If I fussed over my smeared mascara or bags under my eyes, I'd never leave the room.

When I returned to the living room, I found Cameron asleep on the floor, surrounded by hundreds of documents printed and laid out. I chuckled, and warmth spread through my body. He stayed over, probably stayed up hours going over these files.

I knelt beside Cameron and whispered in his ear, "Time to get up sleepyhead."

Cameron jolted awake and wiped away drool from the corner of his mouth. His eyes bulged from his head. "What? What did I miss?"

I burst into laughter. "Nothing. You fell asleep. Why don't

you get a little more sleep? You can crash in my bed if you like?"

He rubbed his eyes. "No, I'm awake now. Thanks, though."

After a few cups of coffee, most of the documents sported neon Post-It notes. We color-coordinated the documents based on the timelines of the mission and the players involved.

Operation Zoo Closure
Case Officer: Benjamin Hammlin
Lead Undercover officer: Zachary Lange
Mission Start Date: May 21st, 2018
Mission End Date: To Be Determined

I didn't know Ben Hammlin too well; he was in narcotics, and I was in homicide. Zac got along with him well enough. I know they squabbled from time to time and didn't always agree, but Zac was able to put their differences aside when it came to working together. He may have disagreed with Ben's politics, choice of whiskey, and even his taste in women, but when it came to nailing the bad guy, they were always on the same page. I wished more than anything I could speak with Ben, get more information on what went wrong, but unfortunately, Zac wasn't the only officer to lose his life that day.

I still remember as if it were yesterday; it was an abnormally warm day in November. The leaves turned a candy-apple red and littered the streets as Ashford longed for the past summer days instead of the looming winter ones to come. The leaves, crunchy and lonesome, tumbled down the streets of the city as if they had a purpose and a place to go. Electricity surged in the air despite the post-Halloween excitedness having expired.

I was on duty that day. A triple homicide happened only a few blocks away. My crime scene fell on the outskirts the Jagged Edges' territory in Ashford. When I heard additional gunfire, my heart stopped. Anytime I heard shots, I thought of

Zac. Where he was, what he was doing. I always feared for his life, but even more so while he was undercover.

I left the scene without a word, despite Dennison calling after me. Dispatch on the radio called for backup. They said an officer was down. I pushed through the perimeter and saw Zac on the ground, his clothes soaked in blood. Ben kneeled beside him, tears streaking his cheeks. Other officers tried to pull me off him, but I hovered over Zac as my body shook with wretched sobs.

"I'm sorry, Elle. I tried to save him. I tried. I tried. I tried."

Ben tried to save Zac from whoever killed him, but he failed.

It didn't take long for my living room to look like an episode of *Homeland*. I sat cross-legged near the beginning of the paper trail. Without messing up the order of the documents, I started scanning them. Zac wrote a profile on all the major game players.

My eyes glanced at each one, but couldn't find the one I wanted to spot: Tiger's. My shoulders slumped as I sipped my coffee.

Maybe Zac wasn't able to get as close to him as he wanted. Or—he got too close.

I couldn't shake my disappointment.

It's still early, I reminded myself.

I checked the time and jumped; it was already eleven in the morning.

I need a shower. And a proper meal.

"I need to clean myself up," I said.

"Me too," Cameron replied. He left the apartment and promised to give me a call soon.

I heaved myself off the floor. Loneliness crept in as the only sounds in the apartment were the meek echoes of my footsteps.

After my shower, I returned to the files in the living room.

One document caught my eye as it didn't have a colored Post-It note attached to its front. The man in the picture looked wildly familiar. I knew I'd seen him somewhere but couldn't put my finger on it.

Malcolm Reed, 27

Lower-level dealer

Territory: West of 27th Street

Background: Born and raised in Ashford. Family has political ties. Rising in rank in the Jagged Edges. Cozy with gang leaders. Try to get more information from him; he's a valuable source.

Political ties?

Malcolm seemed familiar, but I couldn't quite place him. I racked my brains and stared at his picture for what felt like hours. I wondered if maybe I met him in college? Or did I arrest him before I became a detective? Then, it hit me: I never met Malcolm, but I'd met his brother, River Reed, Chief of Staff to the Ashford Mayor.

"Elle, it's so nice to see you!" River kissed both my cheeks, his five o'clock shadow's stubble irritating my skin.

"You, too, River. Successful re-election campaign, huh?"

"Seems to be the case!"

Myself and several other Ashford Police officers stood outside City Hall where John Johnson planned to address the city and reclaim his proverbial throne as mayor. Johnson won by a landslide and promised to continue funding arts and music programs in our schools and continue the fight against organized crime in the city. Mostly everyone in Ashford adored him, with his lion mane of hair and his rotund belly. His family legacy consisted of generations of Johnsons in local, state, and national governments. There were rumors that after his next mayoral stint, he'd run for congress or even governor.

As a show of support, the captain urged the department to attend his speech. Zac, still undercover, couldn't attend, but here I was standing next to River Reed, the mayor's Chief of Staff.

River, no taller than me, was slimier than an electric eel. I wouldn't trust him as far as I could throw him. I always played nice, though. Better to have a decent relationship with the mayor's office than a sour one.

"Well, see you later. It was lovely to see you again, Elle." He stalked away with his chest puffed out and his nose raised. He waved to several people on his way to the podium as the speech was scheduled to begin shortly.

I glanced again at the photo of Malcolm, a mugshot. His pupils were larger than life and centered within his bloodshot eyes. He'd been arrested several times on drug charges, but always managed to wiggle out of them. No doubt because of his brother. What struck me as odd, however, was that before this moment, I had no idea River's brother was involved with the gangs in Ashford. How did he manage to cover that up? Surely it wasn't a good look for the mayor's chief of staff to have familial ties to a criminal. It was something I'd have to ask River the next time I saw him, which I predicted wouldn't be too long at all.

TWENTY-FIVE

L ater in the day, Dennison called me. "How's it going, Captain?"

"Good. Heading to dinner soon. Just wanted to check in and see how you're doing on the Morrison case. I read your report on Orlando. What's your next play?"

I bit my lip. As much as I wanted to focus on finding Tiger and looking into Zac's files, I needed to focus on Emilee's case first. I was the one who asked it be reopened, so it was my responsibility to see it through.

"I'm thinking of talking to Adam's cousin, and maybe talk with Emilee's parents. I know they were interviewed, but I'd like to meet them."

"Keep me updated," Dennison said and hung up.

I texted Cameron and told him I'd pick him up in less than twenty minutes. Even though it was a weekend, the work didn't stop based on the days of the week. He replied with a thumbs up emoji.

"So, where we headed first?" Cameron asked as I pulled away from his townhouse in a small residential district outside of downtown Ashford.

"I figured we'd go to her parents' first. I read their interviews in the file, but at the time, they were so distraught, they weren't able to provide much information."

Cameron agreed and looked up their address. "It's about an hour away."

I put the address into my GPS and jumped on the interstate. Cameron reviewed the file and read the parents' statements to become more familiar before we spoke to them. The interstate wasn't too busy, and we were making excellent time. We'd probably beat the GPS's ETA, something I loved trying to do on road trips.

"Looks like they aren't a huge fan of Adam," Cameron said.

I shrugged. "Can't imagine many parents would be. He's got track marks for days."

"I wonder what she saw in him," Cameron said. "I mean, I get they were first loves and shit, but he didn't bring much to the table."

I rolled my eyes at the crassness of his comment. Speaking of first loves, I couldn't judge too heavily considering mine tried to kill me. Did Emilee's first love kill her too?

"Who was your first love?" I asked.

"Damn, going personal, Dahlia?"

"Just trying to kill some time," I said.

Cameron stayed silent for a few minutes before he cleared his voice. "I don't talk about this stuff with anybody."

"I'm not just anybody."

He groaned. "You're nosey."

"Yup. Now spill."

He looked outside the window. "I was seventeen. Her name was Beth."

"Go on," I urged.

"We were together for about six months before she moved.

We tried to make it long distance, but we were kids. It wasn't meant to work out."

"That must have been tough," I said.

"I got over it. Met Hanna. And then, you know, ended up alone again."

I swallowed hard, knowing all too well how it felt to be living your life, happy and fulfilled, and then it was like a train accident, deadly and sudden. Who would even think to prepare for something like that at such a young age?

"She was pregnant," he whispered.

I swerved to avoid a car that cut us off. My stomach plummeted as I tried to process his words. I waited patiently for him to continue, my heart shattering for him.

"But when her cancer came back, and she started treatment, we knew it would end the pregnancy. It was the hardest decision we ever made, but we agreed she'd fight like hell to beat the cancer again, and then we could try again. But we never got the chance."

"Cameron—"

"Don't. It's okay."

I put my hand on his, but he pulled away, folding his hands in his lap. I put both hands back on the steering wheel, and we drove in silence the rest of the way to Emilee's parents' house.

They lived on a farm they purchased once Emilee went off to college. It was quite the change from New York City where they raised their only daughter. We pulled onto the winding dirt road and parked beside a black Mercedes and a four-wheel drive SUV.

Emilee's parents sat on a bench swing beside the front door. Their porch extended around the house, as far as I could tell. They gazed quizzically at the unmarked car in their driveway.

Cameron and I got out of the car. I waved as we approached the porch. "Mr. and Mrs. Graham?"

"Yes?" Mrs. Graham answered, holding a tall glass of pink lemonade.

"We're with the Ashford Police Department. I'm Detective Dahlia, and this is my partner, Detective Hanover. We're hoping to borrow a few minutes of your time to talk about your daughter."

The couple looked at each other with saddened expressions, but eventually agreed.

Mrs. Graham led us into their home, where family photos and pictures of Emily lined the walls. The decor was a comfortable rustic chic that reminded me of Lisa's wedding venue out in the country, not too far from here. We sat at their kitchen table.

"Can I get you some lemonade? Water?"

"No, thank you," Cameron said.

Mrs. Graham appeared crestfallen but claimed a seat beside her husband. "Adam said the case has been reopened. Is that true?"

"Yes, Mrs. Graham. We're the leads on the case, and we're hoping to bring Emilee's killer to justice."

Mrs. Graham winced.

"So you don't think she committed suicide?" Mr. Graham asked.

"No, sir. We don't."

He clicked his tongue. "Took you all long enough. We told you she didn't do that!"

Mrs. Graham covered her husband's clenched fist with her hand and squeezed. His cheeks turned red, and Mrs. Graham flicked away a tear.

"Can you tell us about Emilee? What kind of person she was? Hobbies? Anything that might help us learn more about her?"

Mrs. Graham stood abruptly and disappeared from the kitchen, but her husband said,

"Our Emilee was a miracle baby. My wife and I tried and tried and eventually gave up on having children. Then, after a cruise to the Bahamas, Kelly found out she was pregnant. When Emilee told us she and Adam were having trouble getting pregnant, we told them to keep trying. That one day, she'd get her miracle baby too."

Mrs. Graham returned with an armful of photo albums. She set them atop the kitchen table and grabbed the one with the least amount of dust. She opened the auburn album and turned it toward us. In the first picture was Emilee and Adam at their high school graduation, wearing gold caps and gowns. Emilee smiled at the camera, her eyes sparkling quite the contrast from the last picture I saw of her in the morgue.

Adam looked more or less the same. He didn't smile for the camera. Instead, he wore a punchy smirk, puffing out the ring inside his lip. Emilee's gown was covered with tassels, ropes and pins.

"She was the Valedictorian," her mother said.

Adam didn't wear any distinguishing items around his neck.

"How did you feel about her relationship with Adam?"

Darkness filled Mr. and Mrs. Graham's eyes. "He wasn't our first choice for our baby girl," Mr. Graham said. "She deserved better."

"He didn't let her have her freedom. She couldn't go out for girls' nights or go shopping on her own without his approval," Mrs. Graham said.

"Why did she put up with that?" Cameron asked with venom in his tone.

"We wish we knew. We tried talking to her. When he proposed, we didn't want to ruin the moment, but asked her if it was what she really wanted."

"Do you know anyone who would want to hurt her?" I asked.

Mrs. Graham flipped through the photo album, stopping on a page that she turned toward us. It was a photo of Adam and Emilee on their wedding day. They married in her parents' backyard to save money. Even though the Grahams appeared to be wealthy, the wedding seemed more casual from the photos.

The photo Mrs. Graham pointed to was of Adam and Emilee cutting the three-tiered cake. Adam's cousin Kyle stood in the background of the photo with the rest of the guests, staring at the couple with his lips turned upward.

"That whole family scared the shit out of me. Pardon my French," Mr. Graham said.

"What about Adam's parents? Where are they?"

"They live in Vegas," Mrs. Graham said. "Adam doesn't see them often. I think they were tired of him begging for money, so they cut off communication."

Mrs. Graham flicked away a tear and turned page after page of the photo album. My heart ached for the Grahams. It was one thing to lose a child and quite another to have one murdered.

"One last question, Mr. and Mrs. Graham. Did Emilee have any history with mental illness? Is there any reason at all you think it's possible she committed suicide?"

"No chance at all," Mr. Graham said firmly. "I know all parents would say that, but Emilee was our pride and joy. She was a happy person. Sure, they had their struggles, but she wanted to live. She wanted to start a family."

"Thank you for your time. We'll be in touch," Cameron said.

We walked out of the Grahams' house. Inside the car, I turned the key in the ignition.

"I think it's time we pay Kyle Morrison a visit."

TWENTY-SIX

We parked outside a high-rise apartment complex that housed people with government assistance. The brick building was decades old and looked it too. I locked the car twice, just to ensure it was secure. A group of young men sat on the stoop by the entrance of the building. The smell of marijuana permeated the vicinity. As soon as Cameron and I approached the men, they stubbed out their spliffs and flicked them into the bushes. Not that we didn't already know what they were doing; we were cops after all.

"Evening, gentlemen," I said like an all-knowing teacher about to bust her students.

A few of the kids snickered, but one greeted us in return. Cameron eyed them suspiciously, but they weren't afraid of him.

We ventured past them and into the building. The notes from Kyle's initial interview relayed the address of his apartment, which happened to be on the tenth and top floor. Cameron and I rode the elevator, which shuddered and shook on its way up. The carpet of the elevator was covered in geometric shapes, worn down by years of residents standing on its surface. The elevator came to a jolt as we reached the tenth floor. I grabbed on to the side until my balance returned.

"You okay?" Cameron asked with a sly grin.

"Yeah. Just not a fan of old elevators. Fuck off," I replied playfully as I rolled my eyes.

"Just checking, Dahlia."

We reached Kyle's front door. I swallowed hard as Cameron knocked on the door three times.

"I'm not interested!" a voice hollered from inside.

"Ashford PD," Cameron exclaimed.

Footsteps shuffled on the other side of the door. Metal clanged from inside and then the door opened.

"Let me see your badges," Kyle demanded through the crack in the door.

Cameron and I whipped out our identification. Once satisfied, Kyle let us inside. The apartment smelled of cigarette smoke and pizza. Dozens of empty beer bottles lined the kitchen counter. Floral wallpaper peeled along the hallway to the living room. Kyle flopped onto his moth-eaten couch and put his feet up on the table. He had a buzzcut, like his cousin, and greenish-gray eyes. He sported flame tattoos up his arms and covering his neck. He wore a Disturbed band t-shirt with black Converse sneakers.

"What's up?"

Cameron sneered. "We need to speak with you about Emilee Morrison."

Kyle sat up straight, his body stiffening. "What about?"

Cameron and I sat on the loveseat across the room. I wrinkled my nose as we took our spots beside each other. Cameron took out his notebook while I pressed record on my phone. "We'd like to know more about your relationship with her."

"She was married to my cousin, but we all met in high school. She was kind of a stuck-up bitch. I told Adam so many times he could do better than a prissy bitch like her."

I cringed at his harsh vernacular. He lit a cigarette and added to the smokey haze of the apartment. Outside, the sun set below the horizon.

"Did you ever argue with her?" Cameron asked.

Kyle looked at us with narrowed eyes. "I didn't kill her if that's what you're asking."

"I'm going to cut to the chase," Cameron said. "We've heard from multiple people there was some resentment that you didn't end up with Emilee—"

"That's bullshit!" Kyle said, knocking over his half-full beer bottle on the coffee table. "Fuck! Look what you made me do!"

Cameron took a step forward, partially in front of me. "You need to calm down."

Kyle looked up, seething. "Are you trying to tell me how to act in my own place, homie?"

"It's Detective Hanover." His face turned ashen as his knuckles gripped the notebook.

Tension filled the air, and I held my breath. A shiver shot down my spine.

"Kyle, where were you on February twentieth?"

"How the fuck should I know?" he asked, wiping the beer spilled on the table with a dirty t-shirt from the floor.

"You should probably find out unless you want to be our number one suspect," Cameron said through gritted teeth.

Kyle stood. "I think I got a haircut that day. Jesus Fuck."

When Cameron stepped toward him, Kyle matched his advances. I bit the inside of my check and stood from the couch.

"Where do you go for a haircut?" I asked.

Kyle looked me up and down, licking his lips. "I go to Slick Willy's. Karl is my guy."

"Great, we'll go talk to him and see if he'll confirm that," I said.

"Why don't we drive down there together? We'll go to Slick Willy's, then I'll show you mine."

Cameron dropped his notebook and stepped toward Kyle with a raised fist.

"No!" I cried.

I lunged toward Cameron and pulled him back. He stumbled a few paces before reclaiming his balance, his fingers trembling over his firearm. Kyle snickered and crossed his arms over his body.

"We're leaving," I said. "Kyle, I wouldn't go on any trips soon. We'll be in touch."

I yanked on Cameron's arm and led him out of Kyle's apartment.

Inside the elevator, Cameron refused to look at me. He clenched his jaw, holding his notebook to his chest. I didn't know what to say. I wanted to scold him for letting his emotions get the best of him. Tell him off for almost hitting a civilian without much provocation. And why did he get so mad, anyway? I could take care of myself. I didn't need a man to defend my honor.

"That was unprofessional," I mumbled under my breath as we got inside the car.

"Drop it," he said venomously.

"Fine."

I dropped him off at his townhome. Cameron didn't say goodbye but slammed the car door shut.

"Good night to you too," I said to myself.

I thought back to the interview with Kyle before Cameron charged him like a bull seeing red. He seemed tense that we asked about Emilee. Did he have something to hide? I needed to talk to him again, but this time, without my partner.

In bed, I looked up Slick Willy's Barber Shop to see it closed two years ago.

TWENTY-SEVEN

The next morning, I decided I needed to run and clear my head. Instead of running the streets of Ashford, I decided to go to Willow Trail Creek instead.

The sun shone brightly as songbirds twittered about in the trees lining the path. Dozens of runners sped past me while I jogged to loosen up. A few bikers with helmets and sunglasses zoomed in the opposite direction on neon race bikes. The dirt path wasn't ideal for my typical workout, but I'd have to get accustomed to it, for today at least.

After a hundred yards or so, I picked up the pace. Sweat trickled down to the small of my back as the rays reached their zenith. I inhaled the summer air, held it in my lungs, and exhaled. There was no better time of the entire year than summer in Ashford. From my fingernails down to my bones, the sunshine fueled my desire to keep going, day in and day out.

Up ahead, a man knelt on the grass beside the path and tied his sneakers. I could spot that neon tracksuit from a mile away: it was River Reed.

He finished with his laces and looked both ways before

resuming his run on the path. Beside us, the creek rushed by; the distinct smell of the water and its earthy accents filled my nose. River didn't notice me as I gained on him.

I watched him as I upped my pace. I didn't see a divot in the path and tumbled to the ground, yelping in pain. "Arrrgh-hghhh! Hell!"

Blood oozed from my knee. River stopped dead in his tracks and whipped around.

In a matter of seconds, he knelt at my side. "Miss, are you okay?"

I looked up with tears in my eyes.

"Elle! Are you okay?" His jaw dropped at the blood streaming down my left leg.

I sucked in a breath and released it through gritted teeth. "Damn it. I'm so freaking clumsy."

He pulled me up and guided me toward a wooden bench a few feet away. I sat down and stretched my knee, hoping it wouldn't scar. A willow tree behind us swayed in the breeze, allowing the rays of the sun to kiss us from the sky.

"Should I call someone for help?" he asked, biting his lip.

I waved him away. "No, no! I'll be fine in a few minutes. Just need to catch my breath."

We sat there awkwardly as he glanced at the path. I could feel his attention swaying to continue his run, so I had to reel him back in. Just when I needed a little luck on my side, I fell face-first into the opportunity to question Reed about his brother.

"It's funny, I was actually hoping to get in touch with you soon. I wanted to talk to you about something, you know, personal."

River gulped and sat straight. A fake smile stretched across his chiseled face. "Oh, do tell."

"I came across a file that mentioned your brother," I said, my voice barely audible.

"Excuse me?" His smile disappeared.

"Yeah, I actually didn't know you had a brother—"

"We don't speak. In fact, he hasn't been a part of our family for a very long time. As you can probably guess, I don't fraternize with criminals." He rose, and I felt the proverbial rug pulled out from under me.

"I need to talk to him. It's important. Do you know how I can get ahold of him?"

River, not looking me in the eye, reached to touch the ground with the palms of his hands. "As I just said, we don't speak. And I'd urge you against contacting him. He's in a bad crowd, and I'd hate for you to get involved."

"It's about Zac!" I called as River turned to the path. "I think Malcolm might know something about Zac's murder."

"Do yourself a favor, Elle. You gotta move on from that. What happened was extremely tragic, but it's over. Let the man rest in peace."

Without a formal goodbye, River turned on his heels and jogged away. I sat there, holding my knee, which had turned a nasty shade of purple, unable to ignore the dread filling my veins. River knew something, and I planned to dig even deeper.

You can run, but you can't hide.

TWENTY-EIGHT

Once the blood congealed enough, I hobbled back to my car. My heart felt heavier the more I thought about my interaction with River. I'd been in the game long enough to know when someone was hiding something. I could feel his deceit and trepidation down to my bones. But now, the bigger question: what was he hiding? Why would he want me to move on and stop looking for Zac's killer? Surely he knew I would never give up without a fight. Unless he *did* know that and was preparing to fight me?

Before I knew it, I reached my car. My heart pumped with adrenaline, and I could barely catch my breath. I needed to go home, though, and clean up. Before I put the keys in the ignition, I checked my phone to see twelve missed calls. Fear seeped into my mind, wondering what was so important that I'd missed. I usually left my phone on silent, but how could I miss it flashing with calls for so long?

I viewed the call log as my stomach churned and my chest tightened. Every missed call, apart from one, was from Adam. Without a second thought, I returned the call, nibbling the inside of my cheek.

"Detective! I've been trying to get ahold of you. I need to talk to you."

"Whoa, Adam. Slow down. Is everything okay?"

"No. Not at all. Can you meet me? I'm at Joe's Deli. I need to talk to you right now."

I glanced in the rearview mirror and cringed at my appearance. But he seemed desperate, so I couldn't say no.

"Okay. I'll be there in fifteen minutes."

He hung up the phone.

Traveling over the speed limit, I cruised to Joe's Deli just outside of Downtown Ashford. The outskirts carried a lot more crime and unsavory people than I voluntarily wanted to submerge myself in. However, I'd heard good things about Joe's Deli, and my stomach rumbled as my shaky hands managed to parallel park a block away from the restaurant. I used the last few fast-food napkins in my glove compartment to wipe my knee, but it was fruitless—my self-induced injury throbbed and couldn't be hidden.

I locked my car, twice just to be sure, then strode toward the restaurant. Overhead, distant dark gray clouds threatened to travel in this direction. Birds twittered about the trees, but an unspeakable threat hung in the air. My palms were sweating, and I wiped them on the back of my shirt, still damp with perspiration from my run.

A few loiterers on the streets, including a group of teens with flashy bikes and a basketball, glanced nervously at me and rode away. Two older men across the street sat in lawn chairs outside a dilapidated barbershop, the red and blue swirling sign catching my eye. Their gaze burned into my back as I felt them watching me. I'm sure they pegged me as a cop the moment I stepped out of my car. But I wasn't in uniform or in an official capacity, just wanted to meet a man who reached out, desperate to see me as soon as possible.

When I opened the door to Joe's Deli, a bell simultaneously warned of my arrival. The black and white checkered floor reminded me of old movies, while several large cracks in the walls were partially hidden by old sepia photographs of patrons throughout the years. In a booth at the back, Adam sat on the edge of the bench with his back to me; I could see his foot tapping against the floor.

I approached him, gently touching his shoulder to announce myself. He jumped as if I electrocuted him. "Hey, hey! It's just me."

His shoulders slumped, but his foot didn't stop jiggling. He wiped his brow with the back of his hand. Our eyes met. I hid my surprise to see his barely visible pupils. I'd heard whisperings around the station that Adam was a user, but I didn't see the signs until now. He'd already had a thin veil of suspicion around him being the husband of a woman who died, but adding drugs into the mix only added to the strikes against him.

"Adam? What's going on? Are you high?"

He looked over his shoulder. "I need your help."

I gulped. "What is it?"

Adam chewed on his cuticles. Blood seeped out from his thumb nail, a nervous habit I knew all too well. "I need money."

"What?" I asked a little too loud.

Adam shushed me while the three other patrons in the deli glanced in our direction. I couldn't see any employees in front of the restaurant, and if I didn't know any better, I would have thought I was in some kind of mob movie.

"The bank repo'd my car today. And I'm a few months late on our mortgage."

"I'm very sorry to hear that. But I can't give you that kind of money. Are you working?"

He banged his head on the table, and I jumped back. "I lost my job after Emilee died. I stopped showing up, so they let me go. No other construction site in the city will hire me."

"I'm so sorry-"

"Isn't there anything you can do? Someone you know who can help me?"

An older woman hobbled through the deli entrance, her hair still in curlers and her walker shuffling by us. A worker at the counter called out her name and greeted her with a hug and kiss on each cheek.

"Adam, I'm a police detective, I'm sure what you expect me to do?"

He sipped his Coke and glared at me, his lip turned upward. "I need more money!"

The wheels inside my mind cranked and turned. This guy was not in his right mind or stable. He was a drug user, unreliable, couldn't hold a job, among other things.

An older man peeled back the plastic separating the dining room from the kitchen. His hair was white as snow, and his hardened look sent chills down my spine.

"What's going on out here?"

"Nothing!" Adam snapped.

The older man looked me up and down and sneered. "I think it's best both of you get going now."

I nodded. "Not a problem."

Adam strode out of the deli before me, letting the door almost hit me in the face.

"Hey, I have another question for you."

"What?" he shot back.

"Do you think Kyle could have had something to do with Emilee's murder?"

"Why would you ever say that?" He clenched his fists at his side.

Because he lied about where he was that day.

"Just wondering," I said.

Adam turned on his heels and stalked down the street, ignoring my calls after him.

"Adam! Wait!"

He didn't turn back.

TWENTY-NINE

W hen I strode into the station the next day, I stopped at my desk to drop off my purse and exchange it for my coffee mug. I poured myself a steaming cup of joe and planned my next move. I didn't have to plan too much, because the very person I wanted to speak with walked right up to me.

"Hey, how are you?" Lisa asked.

"Oh, you know. Same old, same old."

She nodded. "I hear that. I think I watched more Netflix than should be allowed this past weekend."

"Anything good?" I stepped aside and let my former best friend pour her own mug of coffee.

She filled her Harry Potter mug three-quarters of the way full and then doused it with several packets of sugar and powdered vanilla cream. I cringed at the thought of that much sugar in my coffee and could practically feel her cavities.

I remembered all the nights we spent watching movies, gossiping, and baking together. Anytime dessert was involved, Lisa happened to "slip" a few extra teaspoons of sugar. A few times, when reading the recipe to her, I purposely told her less sugar, knowing full well she would add more regardless. I loved her for it, though. Lisa was one of a kind.

"Rewatching *Breaking Bad*. Haven't gone out much since, you know, we separated."

Small talk was great, but I wanted to tell her how I got into Zac's case files from his undercover assignment. I wanted to tell her how desperate I was to find Zac's killer and bring the motherfucker to justice. Instead, I tiptoed around the subject, not wanting to raise any suspicions.

"I was hoping you could help me with something." I followed Lisa out of the break room and to her desk, which was only a few cubes away from mine. She furrowed her eyebrows as she sat in her chair and folded her hands on her lap.

"Yeah? What's up?" She saw right through me.

"I wanted to ask you again if you could put me in touch with Tiger—"

She opened her mouth to interrupt, but I put my hand up, begging her to listen.

"I know you don't want to expose him or put him in any danger, and I promise I won't let that happen. But I need to talk to him about the letter he supposedly wrote to me. Maybe someone is framing him, and he didn't have anything to do with Zac's murder after all, but I need to find out for sure. Please, Lisa. I wouldn't ask if it wasn't important. It's the only lead I have."

She gazed at me and then out of the window. She considered my proposition, as a friend and confidant. She could trust me, even if she didn't fully believe that again.

"You can even be there! I just want to ask him what he knows."

"I'll think about it, okay? That's the best I can do right now. I've spent a lot of time building a rapport with him, and I have to tread extra carefully."

My heart sank, but I understood. "I'm grateful for that, truly. Please let me know as soon as you can, though. Okay?"

"Of course." She turned away and logged into her computer.

I sat at my desk with a lump in my throat. Two cases at the top of my mind, and two cases with barely any leads. I wanted to find out the truth about Emilee, and I needed to uncover the facts about Zac's death and who may have been involved.

Captain Dennison stormed out of his office and pointed at me. "Dahlia. My office please."

Without waiting for me to answer, he turned around. My heart skipped a beat; I knew that tone of the captain's voice anywhere: he was pissed. But what could he be mad about? I hadn't done anything wrong since being back, that I knew of. Did Lisa tell him I was probing into one of her CIs? My stomach plummeted as I imagined this was what it felt like being called to the principal's office. Several officers watched as I followed the captain into his office.

"Close the door behind you," he instructed curtly.

I did as told and took a seat across from him. My heart raced as I crossed my legs and pinched my wrists to try and calm down. I could nearly see steam shooting out of Dennison's ears. "Wha-what's up?"

"I got a call this morning from River Reed."

Motherfucker.

"Oh, what about?"

"Cut the shit, Dahlia," he spat. "He said you accosted him yesterday."

I stood from the chair. "He said what?"

"Sit down," the captain boomed.

I plopped back into the chair while rage built inside of me. "I did not 'accost' him, Captain. I merely ran into him, by coincidence, and wanted to talk to him."

"That's not the story he gave me, and you know we don't need to be making any enemies in politics."

I put my head in my quivering hands that shook with vitriol. "Who are you going to believe?" I asked, my voice barely above a whisper.

His face softened, and his shoulders relaxed. I glanced at a small photo tucked behind others on the cabinet behind him. I knew it was a photo of us on my birthday a few years ago. Zac was in the photo too. My heart throbbed with grief. Things were so simple back then. I was an up and coming detective; Zac's career was blooming too. Things were falling into place, and we were living our best lives.

Little did I know that bliss wouldn't last, and in time I'd hit the bottle and rock bottom. I was better now, though, and I needed to keep getting stronger if I wanted to finally put the past behind me. Until then, it was as if ghosts haunted me day in and day out. Begging me to solve the case. Urging me to find the culprit who ruined my entire life.

"Tell me what happened, then."

My chest heaved a great sigh. I stared at my feet, not wanting to tell him the truth but not wanting to lie either.

"I was out for a jog and we ran into each other. "

"And?" he asked expectantly.

"Well, I've been looking more into Zac's old case files from when he was undercover. There were notes about River's brother, Malcolm. Malcom's deep in the Jagged Edges, and Zac wanted to get closer to him. I only asked River how I could get in touch with his brother to talk to him, and he freaked out." I shrugged.

Captain stood and paced back and forth across his office. He seemed to know something, but wouldn't say it. What was he hiding?

"We can't be bothering Mr. Reed like that. He's off-limits, Dahlia."

"Off-limits? Why? Why can't I ask him a simple question without him running to you like a little girl?"

Captain slammed his palms flat on his desk. I jumped back and clutched my chest.

"Damn it, Elle! Why do you have to be so goddamned stubborn? I need you to listen to me on this, okay?"

I stood from the seat to stare at my boss, friend, and father figure in the eye. "So, you want me to ignore one of the only leads I have to solve Zac's murder?"

"No, I'm simply asking you to leave the mayor and River alone. They don't have anything to do with this. It's not in the department's best interests to be stirring up trouble."

"Sure, whatever you say. I'll leave them alone."

"And what do you mean, one of your only leads? Do you have more?"

I swallowed hard. I was already in deep shit, what more could it hurt to show him the letter supposedly written from Tiger? I pulled out a copy of the letter and placed it on his desk, sliding it closer to him with my pointer finger. I crossed my arms and watched him read it.

"Where did you get this?"

"It was left for me while I was in Keygate. I got it when I finally came home. I'm not totally convinced Tiger wrote it, but I want to find out." I pursed my lips.

My heart sank as he folded the letter and put it in his drawer. Did he care about finding Zac's killer as much as me? Didn't he want to find the person who killed one of our own? My stomach twisted and turned, nausea rippling through me.

"I don't want you investigating this, Dahlia."

"Why not?"

He sighed. "Listen, I'm happy to have you back, but I need to know that you won't tailspin. I'm afraid if you look into Zac's case, you'll lose control again."

My cheeks reddened as shame burned through me. "I'm better now."

"'Now' being the keyword. I'm asking this because I care about you," he said earnestly.

I clicked my tongue.

"Just please leave River alone too. Understand me?"

"You bet."

I walked out of Captain Dennison's office with no intention of keeping that promise.

THIRTY

The day passed agonizingly slow. It consisted of finishing up paperwork and watching the clock. My annoyance from the morning barely dissipated by the time my shift neared its end. Cameron kept his distance throughout the day too. I didn't know what his problem was, and I wasn't in the mood to find out. I hoped he would have cooled off a little bit more since our interview with Kyle.

Both cases' facts swirled in my head. If I wanted to track down Zac's killer, I'd have to be resourceful and exponentially more cunning. Clearly, River Reed wasn't a friend, and unbeknownst to him, he'd turned into enemy number one. Anyone willing to hinder my quest for justice would quickly find out not to get in my way.

"Why're you so quiet today?" I asked as Cameron whooshed by my desk.

He turned, his eyes smoldering. "What's there to talk about?"

"I don't know. You've gone radio silent since we texted last night."

"I don't have much else to say." His nonchalance stung.

Once he walked away, I called Kyle's cell phone after finding his number in the case file. It went to voicemail, and I left a message.

"Hi, Kyle. This is Detective Dahlia with the Ashford PD. I'd like you to come in for a formal interview. It'll just be you and me this time." I hoped that'd be enough incentive for him to return the call. I wanted to ask him face-to-face why he lied about going to the barbershop the day Emilee died.

A few desks away, Lisa collected her belongings and lazily walked toward the door. While she was still in sight, I texted her:

Meet me in ten at our old spot.

Lisa reached for her phone, glanced at the text, and looked briefly at me over her shoulder. She nodded curtly and retreated to the parking lot. I glanced over at the captain, who worked with his door open. He appeared to be focused on something on his computer screen. I didn't bother saying goodbye but instead snuck out of the station before he could notice I was gone.

As soon as I stepped outside, the sun kissed my face with its scorching rays. I dug out my Ray-Ban sunglasses from my purse. Glancing at my phone, I saw I had a few minutes until Lisa and I were to meet. Luckily, our old meeting spot was just down the road.

I parked in the street. Lisa sat at our favorite bench in the courtyard of one of the bigger banks in Ashford and stared at the fountain at the center. I scooted next to her, and she smiled weakly.

"So, you got the brunt end of the stick today, huh?"

"Sure did."

"What was all that about?"

I took off my sunglasses and nudged them on top of my head. I, too, gazed at the fountain, mesmerized by its simplicity and tranquility. A few kids leaned over the edge to drop coins and feel the splash of the water against their faces. I cracked a smile as a young girl with blonde pigtails threw a penny up as high as she could throw and dazzled as gravity pulled it back to earth. It splashed with a distinct *kerplunk* in the water, and she begged her dad for more.

I crossed my arms. "I ran into River Reed and asked him a few questions about his brother, who I think Zac knew from being undercover."

Lisa whistled. "River Reed is such a slimy prick. So he ran to the captain and told on you?"

I nodded.

"What a bitch. I'd love to tell him how I really feel."

"Oh yeah?" I snickered. "Didn't you two date in college?"

"Unfortunately. Then, he got drunk at the inauguration and tried to feel me up. He's lucky I didn't dislocate his shoulder like I wanted to."

We laughed together, and for a moment, it felt like old times. Like nothing ever happened between us, and no bad blood ever emerged. But, as soon as it came, the feeling left the same way.

"So, you still going to try to contact River's brother?"

I tilted my head and looked at her knowingly. "What do you think?"

She chuckled. "Elle Dahlia: stubborn as a damn mule."

"Will you still help me? You know, connecting me with Tiger? I may not get ahold of Malcolm to press him about Zac. And I'm starting to think Tiger may not have written the letter after all, but I want to ask him why someone would want to impersonate him."

"What made you change your mind?"

"When I looked it over again, the handwriting seemed inconsistent. I don't know why someone would want to frame him for Zac's death, but I have to find out."

Lisa looked toward the fountain, her gaze turning cold as

the first winter's frost. "I don't know, Elle. I'd be risking my relationship with my CI, and now that it's on Captain's radar, I'd be putting my career on the line too."

My shoulders slumped, and I leaned forward, my elbows on my knees. "Listen, I wouldn't ask unless it was a thousand percent necessary. I need you, Lisa. I don't know where else to go or where to look right now."

Lisa looked at me from the corner of her eye and bit her lip. "Okay."

My heart skipped a beat as elation coursed through my body. "You will?"

"Fuck it. Why not? I know you'd do the same for me."

I pulled Lisa into a bear hug, and even though she pretended to struggle, she let me cling to her and the newfound hope for a few more seconds.

"Thank you. Thank you! You have no idea how much this means to me!"

"Well, don't thank me yet. Tiger still has to agree to it."

"But you'll do your best to convince him, right?"

She nodded and pulled out a burner phone from her blazer pocket. She pressed her pointer finger to her lips as she dialed a number by memory.

"Hey. It's me. Listen, I need to see you. No, nothing's wrong, but something did come up, and a friend has a few questions for you."

She rolled her eyes and stood from the bench. She trotted away with the phone to her ear, far enough away to where I couldn't hear her any longer. She spoke with her other hand in wild gestures. I couldn't help but grin at her animated ways. I used to tease her for it, but now I sat in awe of her tenacity to help a friend who probably didn't deserve it. I hoped this would be a step in the right direction of mending our friendship. I'd do anything to get her to forgive me.

She puffed out her chest and sneered at the phone as she

hung up. Lisa strode back to the bench with an exasperated expression. "He's not happy and sketched out as fuck."

"Oh?" My stomach dropped like the Tower of Terror.

"But he said he'd meet you."

"You're kidding me?"

"Nope. But he said it has to be tonight."

"Perfect."

THIRTY-ONE

In the past, Lisa and I would have gotten ready together. Sat side by side to do our makeup and helped each other straighten our hair. Tonight wasn't like old times.

I didn't usually go crazy with makeup; I liked a more natural look. But I was going to a bar to talk to Tiger, so I don't want to look like myself. Or even look like a cop. I straightened my hair until it was poker thin, delicately put on a pair of false lashes I picked up at the corner drugstore, and put on enough eyeliner to make me look like a raccoon. I doused myself in perfume from Victoria's Secret and, lastly, dug out my hoop earrings from college.

Once I finished my look, I studied my reflection and couldn't help but laugh. Zac would have no doubt been appalled at my makeup. He'd toss a washcloth at me with a smirk. I missed him so damn much it hurt.

As far as clothing, with some difficulty, I pulled on my tightest jeans after I put on a cheetah-print one-piece Lisa let me borrow years ago.

"I gave Tiger an idea of what you look like. You're going to sit at the bar and order an old fashioned. That'll be the signal, so he knows it's you."

"Where are you going to be?"

"I'll be outside in the car. If I have to come in for any reason at all, I'll have your back. Oh, and here. Use this." Lisa handed me a burner phone almost exactly like the one I used to trap Noah. For a moment, I wondered how that bastard was doing, rotting in jail.

"You good?" Lisa asked.

"Golden."

I turned to Salem, who purred on the bed. "Well, what do you think?"

He stared at me unblinkingly.

"Yeah, I think I look damn good, too."

I scratched behind his ear and kissed him goodbye. I glanced at a photo of me and Zac on our dresser.

I'm doing it, baby. I'm going to find out the truth.

I locked up behind me and skipped a few steps as I raced down the stairs. The older man from across the hall did a double-take when he saw me in the lobby. I didn't stop for chitchat and walked out of my apartment building with my head held high. Big things were happening tonight; I just knew it.

AT THE BAR, I recognized several of the men in Zac's file of the gang. It must have been their haunt because they looked comfortable and mucked it up with the bartender. It wasn't much of a surprise that several heads turned when I walked in. I hadn't shown this much cleavage since college.

I claimed a stool at the end of the bar. Inside, smoke filled the area as men and women smoked menthol cigarettes, and I even saw a few cigars. Rap music blasted from the low-quality speakers, and a few disco balls hung from the ceiling. A woman behind me screeched with laughter as her date tickled her and then kissed the crook of her neck.

I put my elbows on the bar. Its cloudy glass surface covered hundreds and hundreds of pennies. Half the walls inside were cracked brick and gave off a speakeasy vibe. Maybe back in the day, it was.

The bartender tossed his long dreads over his shoulder and winked at me. "Can I get you a drink?"

I leaned over the bar, and while watching his eyes dart to my breasts, I asked for an old fashioned, just as Lisa advised.

The bartender gazed quizzically at me. "That's some drink for a pretty girl like you."

"Yeah, that's what they always tell me."

While the bartender concocted my cocktail, I played it cool. I casually looked from side to side to see if anyone noticed me and my drink order. I wondered if Tiger was actually here. Wasn't he supposed to make contact right after I ordered?

I pulled out my burner phone and texted Lisa: *Just ordered, no sight of him.*

She replied: *Be patient. He's nervous AF*

The bartender slid my drink toward me atop a cocktail napkin. "Enjoy. It's on the house tonight."

I smiled back. "Thank you!"

I examined the drink while the aromas of bourbon and bitters filled my nostrils. While I licked my lips, my hand quivered as it held the sweating glass. After lifting the drink off the bar, I brought it to my lips and noticed handwriting on the napkin.

Back exit.

I looked at the bartender, who flirted with two women. I glanced around, but in the haze, I couldn't see anyone paying me attention. I left the drink behind. With my black glitter clutch in tow, I squeezed through couples and groups grinding on each other toward the neon exit sign. With one more glance over my shoulder, I opened the door, which led to a dark, wet alleyway.

When the door slammed loudly behind me, the hair on the nape of my neck and arms stood straight. My breathing intensified as I gasped for air. I looked all around, but there was no one in the tight alleyway. A fog hung in the air, and then I heard a crash to my left. I jumped back to see a raccoon struggling to escape a rusted dumpster that reeked of rotting garbage. My knees went weak as dizziness swayed my body. I wanted to flee or hide. Fear spiraled inside my mind as shivers rippled down my body.

Stacks of crates, empty beer bottles, empty liquor bottles, and cigarette butts lined the alleyway. The breeze ruffled drive-thru trash bags into the corners. A shrill voice called out to me, and I stumbled back against the building. I clutched the door handle with my sweaty palms, but it wouldn't budge; it locked from the inside.

"What's up, *Detective* Dahlia," the voice said.

My heart skipped a beat as a man dressed all in black sauntered toward me. He wore black pants, a dark gray hoodie, and in his left hand was a handgun. I jiggled the door handle once more, but it wouldn't open.

The man cackled as he stepped into the dim light of a streetlight not too far away. With each step, more and more of the buttery glow revealed his face and identity. His feet squished as he walked through a puddle.

"Malcolm Reed?"

"The one and only." He smiled to reveal several of his teeth were capped with gold.

"I'm here to meet someone else." My voice shook.

He approached me and stood close enough for me to smell the tobacco on his breath and the stale stench of sweat. "I know who you're here to meet, and I'm here to give you a message."

My body tensed as Malcolm took another step closer. My hands clenched into fists while sweat pooled at my temples. My pulse raced, and I clenched my jaw. Claustrophobia moved in like a boat approaching the shore, heavy and fast all at once.

"What's the message?" my lips trembled. I couldn't see straight.

Malcolm raised his fist and punched me in the stomach. I doubled over and cried out in pain, stumbling to keep my balance as I swayed back and forth. He cocked his arm back again, but when he released the blow, I sidestepped in time. Malcolm's punch hit the brick wall.

He pulled it back and rubbed his knuckles. "Motherfucker!"

He lunged toward me, but I moved swiftly behind him. I locked my arms with his and held his arms over his head. He wriggled against me as my pulse raced and adrenaline coursed through my body. My eyes widened while I held Malcolm in my grasp, my feet planted wide apart for balance. Blood rushed to my head as Malcolm struggled to free himself. He bent forward, and in the next moment, he slammed his head against mine. I let go of him and staggered backward, my vision turning cloudy. Pain radiated in my skull as I slammed against the opposite building.

Malcolm shuffled toward me. "Stay away from Tiger. Stop digging. Stop looking."

"What are you talking—"

Malcolm kicked me in the stomach this time, and I toppled over onto the damp pavement, writhing in pain. A guttural roar escaped my chapped lips. My ears pounded while my throat turned dry. I wanted to pick myself up and hurt this fucker, but my brain told me to stay down, that I couldn't win this fight.

"If I have to tell you again, you won't be able to walk away. You hear me?" Malcolm bent down and glared at me while I lay on the ground, my body shaking with rage. I spit in his face, my heart exploding.

He grabbed my face with one hand and squeezed it until I couldn't see straight. I struggled to get out of his embrace, but his grasp was like the Jaws of Life.

"Do you hear me?"

I nodded, barely, and he let me go. Malcolm disappeared into the night, but if there was one thing I knew for sure, it was that I was getting closer. And I wouldn't stop now.

THIRTY-TWO

I hobbled out of the alleyway and glanced both ways down the dark street. Rap music reverberated from inside the bar. I was sure Malcolm joked with his fellow gang members inside, retelling how he showed that blonde bitch who was boss. Sure, I could have arrested him for assaulting an officer, but that would tip my hand much further than I wanted.

Headlights flashed three times down the block; that was my cue. I struggled to walk even that short distance. Pain ebbed and flowed throughout my body. I was tough, but it didn't mean I couldn't succumb to pain from time to time. It didn't take long for Lisa to realize I was struggling to make it to her, and she pulled away from the curb. I lunged for the car and opened the door as if it were a life preserver in the middle of a hurricane. Mascara streaked my cheeks.

"What happened? Are you okay?"

"Drive. Please."

"Shit, Elle. Tell me what happened." She sped away.

I watched the seedy bar get smaller and then disappear in the rearview mirror. I leaned back in the leather seat. My body was wracked with sobs, and I struggled to breathe.

Lisa rested her hand on my knee. "I'm here for you. Everything is okay. You're safe."

When we reached my apartment, I peered out of the window up to the five-story brick building. Paranoia riddled my thoughts while I struggled to slow my breathing. Lisa waited patiently for me to open up.

"Tiger wasn't there."

The street lamp's glow from across the street illuminated Lisa's puzzled expression. "What do you mean?"

"It was a trap, Lisa. He wasn't there. He sent Malcolm Reed to 'teach me a lesson.'"

"Jesus fucking Christ. I'll kill 'im."

I leaned forward in the seat and put my head between my knees. Lisa rubbed my back like she used to do after a rough day at work. Her fingers moved in circular motions, and my panic dissipated a little bit.

"Are you okay?"

"I will be," I whispered.

"I'm so sorry, Elle. You know I wouldn't have put you in that situation if I thought there was any chance of this happening."

I sat back and waved her away. "I know. I know."

"Motherfucker," she mumbled under her breath. "So, what now?"

"Now I'm going to take an Ambien and try to get some sleep. I have to think about everything and regroup."

Lisa nodded. "Do you want me to stay with you tonight?"

The thought of being alone in my apartment after a night like this sent a shiver down my spine, but I needed to be okay with being alone. I appreciated her offer more than anything, but I had to decline. "Thanks, girl, but I'll be okay."

She narrowed her eyes. "Are you sure?"

"Positive."

I opened the door and stepped out into the night. Parked

cars lined my block while striped awnings of local business shone under the streetlamps and starry night sky. I glanced up at my apartment window and couldn't help but smile; Salem lay curled up in our spot. I wouldn't be alone after all.

"Call me if you need anything, okay? I'll keep my volume up tonight."

"Goodnight."

Lisa waited in her idling car for me to get inside the building and turn on the lights in my apartment. I gave her one more wave from my window before I collapsed, my face pressed against the glass. The coolness of the window helped me focus on the task at hand: getting some rest. Tomorrow was a new day.

EVEN WITH THE AMBIEN, I tossed and turned all night. Visions of Malcolm's gold teeth filled my nightmares as he came back for me. In the dream, he broke into my apartment, confessed to killing Zac and then killed me too.

No matter how many times I woke up and drifted back to sleep, the dream continued until I woke up without an alarm, almost surprised to be alive. Part of me wanted to go for a run to clear my mind, but my abdomen still felt tender to the touch. Malcolm really did a number on me. I wouldn't let him get away with it. One way or another, I'd get him back.

I walked into work a few minutes late and found Cameron waiting for me at my desk. He took one look at me and charged me. "What happened to you? You weren't answering your phone last night."

I pushed past him and sat at my desk, putting my phone and purse inside the top drawer.

Cameron's nostrils flared as he tapped his foot against the floor. "Well?"

"I tried to get in touch with Tiger last night, but it didn't work out."

Cameron clenched his fists. "Who did this to you?"

Apparently, I didn't apply the coverup as well as I'd hoped.

"Malcolm Reed. He cornered me in an alleyway and told me to stay away. To stop digging."

"I'll kill that motherfucker!"

"Whoa there, Camelot. Captain already warned me about getting involved with that family. Doesn't mean I'm going to listen, but also doesn't mean you have to put your ass on the line too."

"I'm your partner, Dahlia. We take care of each other."

I couldn't help but smile, even though it hurt. "You're crazy, you know that?"

"Yeah, I know."

My phone vibrated in the drawer. I pulled it out, and Cameron leaned against my desk, craning his neck to see who was calling me. His shoulders stiffened once he saw the number.

"Kyle Morrison."

I waved him away, but he didn't leave my side.

"Detective Dahlia."

"Hey, there, pretty girl."

I cringed. "I would like you to come in today for an interview."

"No can do. But if you'd like, we can talk at the beach. I'm at Lake Chakatwook."

I shivered. That was where Emilee died.

"I'd prefer if you come to the station."

The phone call went dead, and I glanced at my cell in confusion. "Fucker hung up on me."

"He coming in or what?" Cameron asked.

"No, but he said he's at Lake Chakatwook. I'm going to go talk to him."

"Not without me." Cameron reached over to his chair and grabbed his suit coat.

Captain Dennison meandered out of his office. "Cameron? I want to go over the report you submitted. Have a few minutes?"

Cameron looked from me to our captain and groaned under his breath. "Sure, boss."

I grinned like a child. "Sucks for you!"

Once Cameron disappeared into Dennison's office, I grabbed my phone and keys. Maybe this time Kyle Morrison would tell me what the hell went on between him and Emilee.

THIRTY-THREE

I raced through a yellow light and watched it turn red above me. A car honked, and a middle-aged man gave me the finger after his brakes squealed to a halting stop. I couldn't think clearly. I wanted to find out the truth about Emilee.

I arrived at Lake Chakatwook. Families hoarded the beach by the lake as lounge chairs and striped umbrellas covered the sand by the dunes. The bright sun loomed overhead, nearing its peak for the day. Toddlers waddled around with plastic shovels and beach balls. Teenage girls tanned their youthful bodies and lay beside each other, blasting hip-hop songs from their Bluetooth speakers. A few older folks walked the length of the water, sporting tasteful coverups and smiles.

I wished this wasn't the spot where a woman lost her life. I wished it wasn't a place that would always remind me of death. I wanted to sit on the beach and bask in the beautiful summer day, but I couldn't. And I probably never would.

I scanned the beach looking for Kyle, but the crowd made it nearly impossible to find him. I regretted wearing my jeans and a blazer. After a few minutes of looking for Kyle, sweat pooled at the nape of my neck, and I removed my blazer to reveal a sheer gray top. I pulled out my phone and called Kyle, but he didn't answer. I cursed under my breath. I felt trapped in a globe of misery, like it was storming, but only over me.

Out of the corner of my eye, a group of men shouted at each other. A small crowd gathered around them while other beachgoers turned their heads at the commotion. Immediately, I snapped out of my sunken mood.

Two men screeched at a group of shirtless boys, all with Bud Lights in their hands. One of the men turned to look at the small crowd loitering around them. I recognized him immediately; it was Adam. The other male with him was Kyle.

"Adam!" I called out.

He turned his head, and his ocean blue eyes met mine. With my blazer tossed over my shoulder, I trudged through the sand. The teenage boys dispersed at my arrival, packed up their cooler, and jogged toward the parking lot.

"What's going on here?"

"Those college fuckers started shit with us," Adam said, his voice slurred and shaky.

Out of the corner of my eye, beach security tutted out onto the sand. I saw the look in their eyes, and they were *not* messing around.

"Let's get out of here before you two are kicked out, huh?"

Adam and Kyle looked to me and the hefty men heading toward them. "Sounds good. Let's go."

Adam and Kyle followed me as I led the way to the parking lot. The security team stopped us, and before they had a chance to speak, I interrupted, "Detective Dahlia with Ashford PD. I'll take care of them, okay?"

The older security guard shrugged. "Be our guest."

Adam and Kyle kept at my heels while we walked to my car. I unlocked it with my fob and moved the empty water bottles from my front passenger seat to the back floor. Adam crouched to get in beside me while his cousin spread out in the back.

"What's your address again?" I asked.

I wondered how Adam and Kyle got to the beach in the first place as they didn't mention leaving their cars here.

"576 Hawthorne." Adam twisted his hands and bit at his cuticles as we drove.

Neither one of the cousins spoke until we arrived at Adam and Emilee's house.

Adam's house was in a small neighborhood near the high school. It wasn't the best area in Ashford, but far from the worst. Most of the houses on the block mirrored each other in looks, and I assumed they were built around the same time. Across the street, a group of young boys played P.I.G. and hollered when the smallest boy sank the next basket.

Now was my chance to interview Kyle more about his relationship with Emilee. I knew he was hiding something, but whatever it was, was still a mystery to me.

THIRTY-FOUR

I followed Adam and Kyle into the house. My nose wrinkled once we stepped inside. Stale takeout, cigarette smoke and days-old beer permeated the one-story dwelling. Dirty laundry littered the living room while stacks of mail lay spread across the kitchen counter. The big-screen TV glowed in the dank living room with a Playstation screensaver bouncing around. Several empty grease-stained Pizza Hut boxes lay wide open on the coffee table next to a variety of empty liquor bottles. I'd seen frat houses with a nicer interior than this place. If a woman ever lived here, it would have fooled me.

A Marilyn Monroe clock chimed in the corner, probably the only item left of Emilee that I could see at the moment. Adam shuffled to the faded periwinkle couch and shoved the newspaper editions to the floor nonchalantly. Kyle opened the fridge and cracked open a cold beer.

He turned to me with a smirk. "You want one?"

"No thanks."

"Suit yourself." He grabbed a second beer and brushed past me on the way to the living room. He handed the extra can to Adam, who opened it with ease and let the chilled drink course down his throat. He finished the can and slammed it onto the coffee table. I jumped at the sound and clutched my chest.

The cousins sat beside each other while I chose a chair in the corner of the living room. The blinds let in slim rays of sunshine from the afternoon and created shadows on the drift-wood-colored carpet.

Beside me, there was a stack of mail on the end table. Most of it seemed to be junk mail, coupon flyers, but one particular piece of mail caught my eye. Its return address read Together-ness Life Insurance in Dayton, Ohio.

My heart skipped a beat while I squinted to read it. My lips slightly parted as my eyes scanned the first few lines.

Dear Mr. Morrison,

We are writing to you in regards to your inquiry of your deceased wife's life insurance policy. We are sincerely sorry for your loss; however, at this time, we are unable to pay out her policy. We have obtained the autopsy report, and due to the coroner's conclusion of suicide, her policy is null and void pursuant to section 12 A of the agreement.

Adam was trying to cash in on Emilee's life insurance policy? Did he know he wouldn't be awarded any money if death was ruled a suicide? Is that why he pressed so hard for us to find the killer?

I cleared my throat. I still needed to find out Kyle's alibi for the day Emilee was killed.

"Kyle, I was hoping we could talk one-on-one and finish our conversation from before."

"Anything you want to ask me can be done in front of Adam. But if you want some alone time, I can arrange that." He winked, and my stomach turned.

Kyle bounced his knees up and down, and I looked away when he continued to stare unblinkingly at me.

"Fine. If that's what you want." I turned on my recording app for the interview. "Like I said previously, we've heard from multiple people you had resentment toward Emilee. What was the nature of your relationship with your cousin's wife?"

Adam glanced at Kyle from the corner of his eye. Kyle leaned back against the couch and crossed his legs, putting his hands behind his head. "And, like *I* said, I didn't give a shit about her. Sorry, bro. You could have done so much better than a stuck-up infertile bitch like her."

I sucked air through my teeth as anger bubbled inside me. I clenched my phone tighter, my knuckles turning white.

Adam brought his dirty fingers to his mouth where he chomped on his nails and stared at his feet.

"Then why don't you tell me where you really were on February twentieth?"

"I already told you," he said.

"Yeah, you said you were at a barbershop that closed two years ago. Want to explain that?"

Kyle stared at me, his lips in a tight line. I stared back, waiting for his real alibi, if one existed. I waited for him to spin another lie about his whereabouts that day, but it was becoming increasingly clear he didn't have a good answer.

Adam rocked back and forth like a child. Suspicion prickled down my body while the hairs on my neck stood up. I swallowed hard and wished I had a bottle of water. Something wasn't right here.

Adam stood from the couch and smoothed back his buzz cut with his hands. His body turned rigid as he paced back and forth across the room. He pulled out a pack of Marlboros and lit a cigarette. After inhaling deeply, he blew the smoke out in a tight line. The rays of sunshine coming through the blinds illuminated the smoke, and it hung in the air, intertwining with the warm light.

Kyle placed his hand on the pocket of his jeans, where something bulged, and it wasn't just because he was happy to see me. My hands turned slick as they gripped the arms of the chair. Dread filled my veins, and I got an inkling that I shouldn't be here alone.

"Kyle, where were you the day Emilee died?"

Adam held the cigarette between his lips while he cracked his knuckles nervously. Kyle gripped the object in his pocket. I knew it was a gun, or at the very least, he wanted me to think it was. I checked my phone to see several missed calls and texts from Cameron. At a glance, I saw he asked if I was, where I was, and if I was okay.

I rose from the chair and pulled my car keys out of my back pocket. "We're going to have to finish this at the station, Kyle."

"Are you arresting me?" he snarled.

Adam turned to face me with desperation etched across his face. His eyes, wide and pleading, stared into mine. He was afraid. Afraid for me? Or afraid of his cousin?

I looked at my phone once more. Cameron texted me and called me again.

Dahlia, if you're with Kyle, you need to get away!!! He killed Emilee. We pulled his cell records, and his phone pinged the tower nearest the beach right before Emilee's TOD.

Kyle looked me up and down as if I were a fresh piece of meat. I looked at him like the piece of shit he was.

Kyle killed Emilee.

I could arrest him right now, but it was two on one. Would Adam let me take his cousin in handcuffs? Or would he protect him? Did Adam know his cousin murdered his wife? My heart pounded through my chest. I kept the recording going. I didn't want to miss a second of this.

"So, what's it going to be, doll face? You going to arrest me?" he challenged me. Kyle slowly pulled out his weapon from his pants, just enough for me to see it. I pulled out my gun and pointed it at him.

"Put your hands up. Don't even think of pulling that weapon on me."

Kyle cackled and ignored my demand. "You going to shoot me, Detective Dahlia?"

"I will if I have to," I said through clenched teeth. Adrenaline surged through my body. I wanted time to slow down and speed up all at once.

Adam paced back and forth as he lit another cigarette, then he chugged the rest of a beer on the table. Out of the corner of my eye, I saw a black ski mask and a pair of ripped jeans. They looked oddly familiar, and then I remembered where I'd heard about them. My heart skipped a beat.

The bank robbery! The missing pieces fell into place. There were two perps at the bank, and two men stood before me—one brave enough to pull a gun on a law enforcement officer. What were the odds Kyle and Adam robbed the bank? They seemed pretty damn good. If Adam was desperate enough for money to try and cash in Emilee's life insurance policy, he could be desperate enough to rob a bank.

Kyle caught me glancing at the ski mask and jeans. His eyes bulged, and he swallowed hard, momentarily dropping his tough guy persona.

"So, you robbed the bank and murdered Emilee?"

"You don't have any proof, bitch," Kyle snarled.

"I'd say those clothes are pretty solid proof. We have several eyewitnesses who recalled that's what the robbers were wearing."

"Bullshit," Kyle spat.

"Why did you do it, Adam? Did he make you rob the bank?"

"I didn't make him do shit!" Kyle said.

Adam's hands quivered as he held his cigarette. He looked to me pleadingly.

"Did you know he killed Emilee?" I whispered.

Tears streaked down Adam's face. He stalked toward the wall and punched a hole through it.

"He said she deserved it," he cried. "She was cheating on me. Maybe she faked her miscarriages too!"

I jumped back, my gun still trained on Kyle. My chest rose and fell as my breathing intensified. Sweat soaked through my top, which clung to my back. I wanted to call for backup, but I knew I had to keep my gun trained on Kyle, otherwise I might as well sign my death sentence.

Sirens crooned in the distance.

They must know where I am. Or think I could be here. In a few minutes, backup would arrive. Adam and Kyle would be arrested.

Kyle glanced at the patio door as the sirens grew louder.

"Don't even think about it!"

Kyle smiled slyly and pulled out his gun. In the next second he pointed it upward and shot the ceiling fan above us, sending it careening to the floor. I ducked and leaped out of the way just in time as the fixture fell in front of me. Pieces of the ceiling and dust showered upon us. I crouched on the ground and covered my face. Adam hollered and jumped back against the wall. I peeked through my hands to see the patio door wide open, and Kyle was gone.

THIRTY-FIVE

By the time backup arrived, there was no sign of Kyle. I showed Cameron and Captain the clothing and ski mask. Cameron arrested Adam for robbery and hauled him back to the station.

Captain Dennison drove me to the hospital to get checked out. In the commotion, I hadn't realized a piece of ceiling landed on my head.

"You may have a concussion," Dennison said.

"I'm fine! Let me go back out and help the search team find Kyle," I pleaded.

"Can't. You gotta get checked out."

Reluctantly, I agreed, under the condition I would drive myself.

At the hospital, all I could think about was Kyle getting away. I should have arrested him on the spot. I cursed myself for not being more aggressive, even though deep down, I knew it was two against one, and I would have been foolish to try arresting him on my own.

The ER doctor cleared me and said it didn't appear I had a

concussion, and I was free to go. I tried calling the captain and Cameron to say I was on my way back to the station, but neither answered.

I left the hospital as dusk swallowed the day. A car sped through a red light ahead, its wheels squealing. Exhaustion rippled through me as I crossed the street, now only a block away from my car. I couldn't believe hospital parking was full when I got there. My feet ached and throbbed. I couldn't help but yawn as I pulled my car keys out of my purse, eager to get back to work.

However, the closer I walked toward my car, the more I realized something wasn't right. Shattered glass sprinkled the sidewalk and curb beside my car, glittering under the glowing street lamp above my vehicle. My breath caught in my throat. I forced myself to jog to my car, where I gasped, "What the hell?"

All my car windows were shattered, and glass shone on the seats as well as the car's floor. My glove compartment lay hanging open, now empty. My nostrils flared, and my pulse exploded. My vision turned cloudy with rage. I waited until a car passed by me and stepped to the driver's side. My front left and back left tires were slit. There was no way I could drive it to the station.

I'd call a Lyft, but once I opened the app, the closest car was over twenty minutes away. I couldn't wait that long. I needed to find out what the hell was going on with Adam and if they found Kyle yet. I was only a mile or two from the station. I could walk it.

Cursing under my breath, I called Cameron again. He didn't answer, so I left a message. "Hey, Cameron, it's me. Listen, someone fucked up my car. I need a ride to the station. Can you call me back as soon as you get this? I'm going to walk for now."

I leaned against my car, wondering why anyone would do such a thing. Sometimes, no matter how many steps you progressed to get your life back on track, the universe had other plans in store. I slapped my car with the palms of my hands and cried out.

A woman walking her shih tzu across the street hid her face and scrambled to put distance between us. I shook my head while my hands quivered, still clutching my keys. Overhead, a plane flew by, its roar loud and omnipresent. I checked my phone again, but nothing from Cameron.

Fatigue plagued my body. Huffing, I took pictures of my car for the report I'd file.

Resigning to my bad luck, I pushed off my car. A few restaurants on either side of the street played music while patrons laughed and chatted with each other. What I wouldn't give to be there, with friends and someone I loved; the only tough decision to make would be what to order for dinner.

Even though it was nearly summer, a chill hung in the air. I groaned, wishing the night were ending differently. I checked my phone again, but no missed calls or texts from Cameron.

I crossed the street and narrowly avoided a man on a bicycle who didn't look before zooming by. "Watch it, asshole!"

Irritation filled me to the brim. As traffic and pedestrians dwindled on this stretch of downtown, my footsteps echoed against the pavement and bounced off the shops and offices that were closed for the night.

My phone vibrated in my pocket. I took it out to find text message from Jake.

Hey, Dahlia. You okay? I saw they arrested Adam Morrison. His cousin is still on the loose? Call me.

A brief smile broke out across my face. It was nice to have someone check in on me. I'd call him a little later, after I figured out what was going on at the station.

A second set of footsteps joined mine. A prickle of suspicion traveled down to the small of my back, and I turned around to see a man a dozen or so yards behind me. He hung his head and stared at his boots while he walked, a cigarette in one hand. I picked up my pace, but the stranger behind me did the same. I clutched my keys between my fingers, a trick I learned in self-defense class back in college. If only I had my gun with me, I wouldn't feel a creeping dread dripping into my empty belly. But the captain suggested I didn't bring it to the hospital with me.

I slowed my pace and looked over my shoulder; the man slowed down too. This was a cat and mouse game I wasn't in the mood to play. I stopped dead in my tracks and listened. The man's footsteps stopped as well. I turned around, but the man was gone.

Damn it, Elle. You're just being paranoid.

I checked my phone once more, even though I didn't hear any calls or texts come through. A panhandler sat on the next corner. I walked past him and tossed a few bucks into his frayed baseball cap which lay beside him.

"Thank you, miss," he said through missing teeth and a long graying beard.

"Have a good night."

I waited at the light. A few event posters on neon paper were stapled to the light pole. A street sweeper pulled up behind me, and the man yielded to me so I could cross the street. At the other side, a streetlamp's bulb burned out, and there was a stretch ahead of me with no light, only the swaying trees in the darkness that filtered the moon and stars overhead.

Out of the corner of my eye, the man who followed me returned into my peripheral view. Only this time, he wasn't looking down. My breath caught in my throat as the man, covered in a ski mask, charged toward me, holding a knife. I opened my mouth to scream, but he covered it with a gloved hand.

He held the knife to my back. "Good evening, Detective Dahlia. Wanna have a chat?" Kyle asked, then dragged me off the street and into a dark alleyway.

THIRTY-SIX

K yle grabbed my left arm and covered my mouth. The cheap fabric of his gloves tasted of dust and cigarettes. I wriggled in his grasp, but the harder I fought against him, the tighter he held on to me. His fingers squeezed hard into my bicep. We stepped over tattered blankets, and I nearly tripped on a splintered wood pallet.

Newspaper sheets ruffled in the breeze. A black and white sign against the wall read Loading Area, and I stepped onto a tossed away needle. I cringed as the sharp point stuck through my shoe and pierced the skin on my heel. I opened my mouth to cry out, but no sounds escaped. I could scream for my life, and no one would be the wiser; they wouldn't hear me.

He pushed me up against the wall and pressed the knife against my abdomen. My chest rose and fell in rapid succession.

"If you scream, I will kill you. Do you understand me?"

I nodded while blood pumped in my ears. I could only see his eyes and his chapped lips through his mask. He smelled like stale beer and sweat.

"Kyle," I breathed.

A sly grin spread across his face. "Missed me, baby?"

A car drove by. No streetlamps could reach us while we were hidden in the shadows. My breath caught in my lungs; I couldn't breathe. My lips trembled, and I felt the color drain from my face, turning it ashen and pallid. My leg muscles tightened, wanting to break free and run as far away as I could from my captive.

"What do you want from me?"

"I want you to get me a deal."

The knife prodded into my belly, and I gasped.

Kyle grunted. "I want a deal."

My brain buzzed with confusion and delirium.

"You're not getting a deal, asshole. I have Adam on record saying you killed his wife. You're going away for a long time."

He pushed the palm of his hand against my throat.

"Go ahead. Kill me. You won't get away with it."

I chomped on the inside of my cheek. My pulse pounded. Distant music sounded from downtown, and cars continued to drive by, ignorant of my situation in the alleyway.

Kyle grabbed my cheeks with his hand and squished my face together. I struggled against his grasp, but he was too strong. Even with all of my self-defense classes and training with Rami, I was powerless against this man. If I struggled too much, he'd kill me. Then again, if I did exactly as he told me to, he could kill me regardless.

"I'm not the DA. I can't cut you a deal."

"Well, you better figure it out. Or else I'll be visiting your mom and stepdad back in Keygate. You know, it's far too easy to find out about someone these days with the internet." He grinned maliciously. "You look just like her."

My body tensed, and I pushed back against the brick wall, even though its grainy texture dug into my skin. Time froze, and for a moment, I stood there, my knees buckling. I tried to back away, but I was already pinned against a building. A lump formed in my throat. My limbs turned heavy, numb.

Kyle inhaled the cigarette he lit and held the smoke in his lungs for a few seconds before blowing it into my face again. He still pointed the knife at me. I was defenseless.

Heat rose to my cheeks, and I clenched my quivering fists. "Adam knew you killed her, but he wanted the insurance money. Didn't he think that if we opened the case, the clues would lead to you?"

"We hoped that once the case was open, the insurance company would pay up," he said bitterly. "Then, we'd get the hell out of dodge and go underground with the cash."

"You loved her though. Why would you kill her if you loved her?"

"I thought I did," he growled. "I thought I was in love with her, but she chose Adam over me. And then she cheated on him. She was good for nothing."

"So, you killed her because she cheated, then once you realized Adam was broke, you decided to rob the bank?"

"You're smarter than you look, little piggy."

"How'd you do it?" I croaked.

Kyle cackled. "It was so damn easy! I stopped by the house and told her I knew about her affair and that I was going to tell Adam. She tried to call my bluff, said she'd already told Adam, but I knew that wasn't true. She was a coward. I told her the only way I wouldn't tell him was if she met me at the lake so we could talk more."

"You blackmailed her," I hissed.

Just like he wants to do to me.

Kyle waved me away. "Yeah, whatever. Anyway, she got to the lake first. And everything was just so fucking perfect. She was in the water when I got there. She made it too easy for me. I eased into the water and followed her in. We were alone. She went under the water, and I came up behind her. Pushed her down. She struggled, but I was stronger. It was the best fucking feeling ever. I was protecting my cousin, my best friend. She deserved to die. She couldn't give him a baby, and she couldn't even be faithful to him."

Yes, Emilee cheated. Was she a horrible person? Not that I could tell. People made mistakes, but that didn't mean they deserved to be killed for them. Maybe she was planning to tell Adam? Maybe she wanted to make everything right? Now, she'd never have the chance.

Reality spiraled around me, and I felt I was falling further and further. A shrill call echoed in the alleyway, and I didn't know who it was coming from until Kyle raised his fist and punched me under my right eye.

"Shut up, you bitch! I'll kill you!"

I crumbled to the ground like a rag doll, my phone shattering against the pavement. Tears oozed out of my eyes while I clutched my face. Kyle knelt beside me with his knife drawn.

"Elle?" a man's voice called out.

Kyle looked to me and then to the entrance of the alleyway. He pulled me to my feet and pressed the tip of the blade against my throat.

"Elle, where are you?"

I recognized that voice; I'd know the sound of it anywhere. I wanted to call out, to scream, but I didn't trust that Kyle wouldn't slit my throat if I did so.

"How would someone know where to come looking for you?" Kyle spat.

Cameron finally heard my voicemail. He knew I was walking from the hospital to the station.

The cold, metallic blade pressed farther into my neck, drawing blood. Would Kyle kill me, right here, right now?

Cameron's shadow filled the foot of the alleyway. Kyle

growled a low guttural sound. I stood against him, frozen in place.

"Elle?" Cameron called. He looked down the alleyway to see me and Kyle, blood dripping down my neck.

"Well, look what we've got here, another cop."

THIRTY-SEVEN

"Let her go," Cameron said. He walked into the mouth of the alleyway, his gun drawn.

"Take one step closer, and I kill her." He dug the knife into my throat a little more. I couldn't breathe. I couldn't think straight. Cameron was so close to saving me and yet too far.

"Okay, okay." He stopped his advances down the alleyway and put his hands up in surrender. "Just don't hurt her."

"Toss your gun over here." Kyle ordered.

"It's over, Kyle. Adam confessed to everything. You have a warrant out for your arrest," Cameron said, slowly lowering his weapon.

Kyle pressed the knife's tip against my throat a little harder, drawing more blood. The warm, coppery liquid oozed down my neck. The alleyway, dark and still, allowed for the soft plops of my blood to be heard as they fell to the pavement. Cameron put his gun on the ground with his hands still up in surrender.

"Kick it over here."

As instructed, Cameron nudged the gun a few feet away from him. His body turned rigid as he watched Kyle move me forward so he could reach Cameron's gun. I wanted to scream for help, but I didn't dare. Kyle now had a knife and a Smith & Wesson. I couldn't see how we'd make it out of this alive.

Cars continued to pass the alleyway, ignorant to the standoff ensuing.

"Now, as I told Miss Dahlia over here, this is how it's going to work." Kyle, still gripping my arm, removed the knife from my throat and put it in his back pocket. He put the gun against my back, the cold metal chilling me to the bone.

"You're going to get me a deal, or I'll kill her parents."

"You'll be in jail before you get the chance," Cameron said, baring his teeth.

"You think I don't know people, asshole? I could snap my fingers, and her parents would be dead before she had a chance to say goodbye."

Tears flowed down my cheeks and mingled with the blood on my neck. I clenched my stomach as fear pulsed through me. I never thought my parents would be in danger because of my career.

Cameron ran his hands through his silky black hair.

An ambulance screeched in the distance. Laughter reverberated across the street as a group of people strolled by, arm in arm. I held my breath, wondering if they'd look over. I couldn't breathe as they passed, but fortunately, not one of them noticed. It was for the best, really. There was no telling what Kyle would do if someone saw us. He'd probably kill me and Cameron without blinking.

Above, lightning and thunder cracked. In all the fuss with Kyle, we hadn't realized that a storm rolled in, blocking out the moon and stars in the sky. Thunder boomed once more, and I jumped.

"Fine, we'll talk to the Ashford District Attorney. But you know we have to arrest you first," I said.

The force of the gun into my back lessened, and his grip

slackened on my arm. "Okay" Kyle said, his voice smooth and even.

Kyle relinquished his hold on me and pushed me away. I stumbled into Cameron's arms as my chest rose and fell. Cameron pulled me close and stood in front of me. He checked me over for any other injuries.

"I'm fine; I'm fine. Give me your phone. I'll call it in."

I didn't want to submit to Kyle's demands, but my parents' lives were more important right now.

My mind raced as I fumbled with Cameron's phone, my hands shaking uncontrollably.

"This is Detective Dahlia calling for backup. We have Kyle Morrison. Yes, those are our coordinates. Hurry."

The storm clouds released warm summer rain onto us. It trickled down at first, but intensified until my clothes stuck to my skin. The drops washed away the congealed blood on my neck, the wound stinging at the rain's touch. Kyle stood in the alleyway, also drenched.

"Toss my gun back to me," Cameron said.

Kyle lifted his mask halfway so the lower half of his face was exposed. He looked at the gun, then to Cameron.

I could still smell the cigarettes on his breath and stale beer permeating his clothes. My stomach churned with raw rage. All of this, all of the death and crime was centered around greed and jealousy. A woman, flawed, but not evil, lost her life. Dozens of people were traumatized for enduring a bank robbery conducted by two men desperate for cash. I chased death, and it found me first. Emilee's murderer, the man I searched and searched for, stood several feet away from me.

I wanted to push Cameron aside and charge the bastard. I wanted him to pay for what he did. He deserved to be dead, or worse, locked up for the rest of his life. And as much as I felt for Adam too, he wasn't innocent in this.

Then, a woman with fiery hair and a look of determination stood at the front of the alleyway with her gun drawn.

"Put your hands up, asshole!" Lisa shouted.

"Lisa!"

"I just heard the dispatch call. I was down the street and figured I'd answer."

Kyle didn't lower Cameron's weapon but pointed it at me and Cameron. My heart pounded. I dug my nails into Cameron's arm, but he didn't flinch.

"I said, lower your weapon now!"

Kyle smiled and pointed the gun at Lisa. A gunshot rang out, and another. Cameron and I fell to the ground. It was as though time slowed, and we hung in limbo before we hit the pavement. Cameron crushed me as he fell on top of my body. Then another body dropped to the ground with a hard thud.

All I smelled was blood and smoke.

THIRTY-EIGHT

The even beeps of the heart monitor lulled me to sleep that night, despite the stringent scent of sanitizer and latex gloves permeating the room. While I tossed and turned all night, I believe I managed a few hours of rest before a doctor was paged over the intercom. I roused, felt for the bandage across my neck, and slowly opened my eyes.

The pale eggshell walls looked better in the daytime, and the HD TV hanging from one played the morning news on mute. An array of flower arrangements, extra pillows, and blankets lined the windowsill.

Cameron and I were able to share a room, the second time I was in the hospital in two days. I listened to his even breaths.

"Fuck," Cameron wheezed.

I pulled myself up and leaned on my elbows, craning my next to see him. "Mornin', detective."

"Hi," he said with difficulty.

"Are you in pain? Do you want me to call the nurse?"

Cameron nodded weakly and moaned.

All things considered, we left the alleyway with minimal

damage. Kyle managed to fire Cameron's weapon, but only hit him in the shoulder; it was a through-and-through shot. He'd fully recover in no time. Kyle, however, wasn't so lucky. Lisa shot him only moments after he'd fired the gun, but he was dead before his body hit the ground. Lisa was an excellent shot.

I rode in the ambulance with Cameron. He took it like a champ, even though he repeated he was fine over and over again through gritted teeth. How could I ever repay him? He risked his life to save me from a lunatic with a gun.

"I'm not going to leave you alone, okay?"

"I'm a big boy, Dahlia," he said through his clenched jaw.

Having solved Emilee's murder felt like a huge weight lifted off my shoulders. Emilee wouldn't come back, even though I'd caught her killer. Nothing could bring her back. But, knowing her soul could finally rest in peace had to be enough. I'd have to let her go.

The nurse entered the room with a cheerful demeanor. She checked our vitals and administered Cameron more pain meds. She promised the doctor on call would be around shortly for morning rounds.

"Oh, you've got a visitor, Elle," the nurse said with a smile.

It wasn't lost on me that it wasn't too long ago I was in the hospital awaiting visitors to check on me after solving a case and catching a murderer.

Jake walked in with a bouquet for daffodils and a Get Well Soon balloon.

"Hey, Jake," I said.

He walked over to my bed and kissed my forehead. "Hey, Dahlia. You're alive."

"Yup, here I am."

Cameron cleared his throat. Jake turned to see my partner in the bed next to me. "Hey. How are you feeling?"

"Fine," Cameron grumbled.

Jake sat in the visitor's chair beside my bed. I told him about the previous day's events and how Cameron saved my life during the standoff with Kyle Morrison.

Jake stood from the chair and walked over to Cameron. My breath caught in my chest. Cameron eyed Jake suspiciously as he approached him.

Jake extended his hand to Cameron. "Thanks, man. Thank you for saving her life. She's really lucky to have you as a partner."

Cameron reluctantly shook Jake's hand. "It was nothing."

Jake didn't stay much longer after that, and I noticed Cameron visibly relax once he left. He turned to face me, his usually perfect hair now a mess from sleeping in the uncomfortable hospital bed.

"So, what's the deal with you two?" he asked casually.

"With who? Me and Jake?"

He nodded.

"We've been friends since college."

"Just friends?"

"Yeah, nosey. Why do you ask?"

"No reason."

Butterflies swarmed in my stomach. Why did Cameron care so much about Jake? Why did he physically turn rigid at the sight of him? Part of me had an idea why, but I didn't want to go down that path.

Outside, the sun shone brightly across the gardens, which we could see from our room. Someone else knocked on the door. I turned to see who was visiting our room this time.

"Kira!" I called.

"Hey!" She walked into the room shyly.

Cameron, now asleep, didn't stir at the arrival of my friend. She nodded toward him and mouthed a question.

"That's my partner," I said, my voice low.

She winked and gave me the thumbs up, but I waved her away. Kira sat on the edge of my bed and held my hands in hers. She wore a pink and blue floral dress and her hair in long braids.

"You're all over the news," she said.

I groaned. "So I've heard."

We spent the next half hour catching up. She mentioned a man from the coffee shop asked her out on a date. She wondered if it was appropriate considering her background.

"Everyone deserves happiness, especially you, Kira. If he can't accept you for who you are, then you'll move on and find someone who will."

"What about you? You dating anyone yet?"

I nibbled on my lip and crossed my arms over my body. "No, I'm not sure if I'm ready."

"Well you won't know if you're ready or not until you try," she said.

"Touché."

We laughed with each other until I turned silent and stared out the window. My stomach in knots, I wrung the sheet in my hands.

"What do you need?" Kira asked.

"What do you mean?"

"I know you, Elle. I know when you're going to ask me for something."

I sighed, my shoulders slumping. "You're right. You know me too well. So, I'm wondering if you may be able to ask around or think back to old friends. I'm trying to find someone."

"I'll see what I can do. Who are you trying to find?"

A trickle of sweat slithered down my temple and wormed its way around the bandage on my neck. Cameron snored next to us while nurses and doctors passed the room holding clipboards and cell phones to their ears.

"I don't want to put you in an uncomfortable or unsafe situation, but I'm trying to find a woman who's dating someone from the Jagged Edges."

Kira raised her eyebrows. "Oh, really? What for?"

"It's about Zac."

I didn't need to elaborate as Kira nodded and put her hand up. "Say no more. Who's the banger?"

"His name is Tiger."

She rolled her eyes.

"You know him?"

"Oh, yeah. I know him, all right. He's a piece of work, he is."

"Do you know his girlfriend? I'm not sure I have her name."

Kira chewed on the inside of her cheek as she placed her manicured fingers under her chin. "I think I know who she is, but I can find out for sure."

"I need to talk with her, in an unofficial capacity."

"I'm on it." Kira stood from my bed and promised to do a little digging.

"Thank you, this really means a lot."

"It's nothing. I'm happy to help. Just like the old days." She winked.

That night, Cameron and I watched a movie in our room. We argued about which one to choose, and we eventually settled on *How to Lose a Guy in Ten Days*. His pain subsided with his latest dose of morphine. He wore a goofy grin and laughed throughout the film. I couldn't help but watch and memorize his movements. He was a man in great physical and emotional pain, and yet he was willing to put himself in front of a bullet for me. I knew we didn't start off on the greatest of terms, but he more than proved his loyalty to me. Maybe he'd make a great partner, after all.

"Hey, Dahlia," he said, a goofy grin on his face.

"Yeah?"

"I'm glad you didn't die." He gazed into my eyes, his own sparkling in the darkness of our room.

"Me too."

GET BOOK 3: CAPTURING EVIL

ALSO BY LAURÈN LEE

ACKNOWLEDGMENTS

Chasing Death came together with a little help from my friends: Rachel, Megan, Emerald, and Kiersten.

As always, thank you, Krista for your amazing editing skills.

Murphy Rae, thank you again for designing the perfect cover for this book and the series.

And, thank you, readers, for continuing to support me. I wouldn't be where I am today without all of you!

ABOUT THE AUTHOR

Laurèn Lee was born and raised in Buffalo, New York, but currently lives on the Space Coast in Florida. She loves hockey, chicken wings and spending time with family, friends and her fiancé.

Reading and writing are her life's passions and becoming an author is her ultimate dream.

As a child, Laurèn became enamored with the Harry Potter series. As an adult, she loves psychological thrillers and mysteries with a twist.

Make sure to sign up for my Email Newsletter to be the first to know about new releases, sales, and giveaways!

For more information…
www.laurenleeauthor.com

facebook.com/laurenleeauthor

twitter.com/laurenleeauthor

instagram.com/laurenleeauthor

Made in the USA
Columbia, SC
30 August 2020

18009545R00131